For Morwenna

First published 2013 by Macmillan Children's Books
a division of Macmillan Publishers Limited
20 New Wharf Road, London N1 9RR
Basingstoke and Oxford
Associated companies throughout the world
www.panmacmillan.com

ISBN 978-0-230-75980-0

Copyright © Chris Riddell 2013

Goth Girl

and the Ghost of a Mouse

CHRIS RIDDELL

MACMILLAN
CHILDREN'S BOOKS

THIS BOOK CONTAINS FOOTNOTES BY THE SEVERED
FOOT OF A FAMOUS WRITER WHO LOST THE
AFOREMENTIONED FOOT AT THE BATTLE OF
BADEN-BADEN-WÜRTTEMBERG-BADEN

Chapter One

Ada Goth sat up in her eight-poster bed and peered into the inky blackness.

There it was again.

A sigh, soft and sad and ending in a little squeak.

Ada looked across the bedroom as she held up the candle and stepped out of bed.

'Who's there?' she whispered.

Ada was the only child of Lord Goth of Ghastly-Gorm Hall, the famous cycling poet. Her mother had been a beautiful tightrope walker from Thessalonika, whom Lord Goth had met and married on his travels. Unfortunately Parthenope had been killed when Ada was still a baby, while practising on the roof of Ghastly-Gorm Hall during a thunderstorm.

Lord Goth never talked about that terrible night. Instead he stayed at home in his huge house, shut away in his study writing extremely long poems. When he wasn't writing, Lord Goth spent his time riding his hobby horse Pegasus, around the grounds and taking potshots at the garden ornaments with a blunderbuss. Before long he had acquired a reputation for being mad, bad and dangerous to gnomes.

Since the accident, Lord Goth had taken to believing that children should be heard and not seen. He insisted that Ada wear big, clumpy boots whenever she walked down the corridors and passageways of Ghastly-Gorm Hall. That way, he could hear her footsteps approaching and avoid seeing her by ducking into his study where he wasn't to be disturbed.

LORD GOTH

This meant that Ada didn't see much of her father, which sometimes made her sad, but she understood. Once a week, when she took tea with him in the long gallery, Ada would see Lord Goth's expression change whenever their eyes met. His look of intense sadness was enough to tell Ada that he was being reminded of her mother, Parthenope, the beautiful tightrope walker, and the terrible tragedy that had occurred. With her black curly hair and green eyes, Ada looked just like her. (Ada knew this because she had inherited a locket with a miniature portrait of Parthenope inside.)

'Who's there?' Ada whispered, a little more loudly this time.

'Only me,' came a small voice from somewhere in the shadows.

Ada slipped her feet into the black leather pumps beside the bed. They were her mother's

tightrope-walking slippers, a little big but very comfortable and, most importantly of all, very quiet. Ada liked to wear them to creep around Ghastly-Gorm Hall. Exploring was her favourite thing to do, especially at night when everyone else was sleeping. Because, even though Ada had lived there all her life, the Hall was so big there were still rooms she had never been into and outbuildings hidden in overgrown parts of the grounds that she had yet to explore.

Ada stepped on to the faded Anatolian carpet, holding the candle out in front of her. There, just visible on a faded patch in the centre, was a small figure, white and shimmering and slightly see-through.

Ada's eyes opened wide.

'You're a mouse!' she exclaimed.

The mouse shimmered palely and gave another sigh that ended with a soft squeak.

'I used to be,' it said with a shake of the head, 'but now I'm the ghost of a mouse.'

GHASTLY-GORM HALL

THE EVEN-MORE-SECRET GARDEN

THE SECRET GARDEN

THE BACK of BEYOND GARDEN (UNFINISHED)

THE OLD ICE HOUSE

THE BROKEN WING

THE UNSTABLE STABLES

THE HOBBY HORSE STABLES

THE ALPINE GNOME ROCKERY

THE VENETIAN TERRACE

'THE WEST '

THE AVENUE OF OUTRAGEOUS FORTUNE

TH

N

E

S

THE SLOUGH OF DESPOND

METAPHORICAL SMITH'S HOBBY-HORSE RACECOURSE

TH HI OF

AM

THE GRAVEL PATH of CONCEIT

THE POND OF INTROSPECTION

THE LAKE of
EXTREMELY COY
CARP

THE
SENSIBLE
FOLLY

THE
DRAWING-ROOM
GARDEN

THE NEW
ICE HOUSE

THE BEDROOM
GARDEN

THE KITCHENS

THE KITCHEN
GARDEN

THE EAST WING

THE DEAR
DEER PARK

THE
OVERLY
ORNAMENTAL
FOUNTAIN

THWARTED
HOPE

FINISHING
POST

START
LINE

TO THE
HAMLET of
GORMLESS

Being so old and so big, Ghastly-Gorm Hall was home to quite a few ghosts. There was the white nun who sometimes appeared in the long gallery on moonlit nights, the black monk who occasionally haunted the short gallery and the beige curate who slid down the banisters of the grand staircase on the first Tuesday of each month. They usually mumbled, wailed softly or, in the case of the curate, sang in a high-pitched lisping voice, but they never actually *said* anything, unlike this mouse.

'Have you been a ghost for long?' Ada asked, putting the candle down and sitting cross-legged on the carpet.

'I don't think so,' said the ghost of a mouse. 'You see, the last thing I remember was scuttling along the corridor of a dusty, cobwebby part of the house I'd never been in before.' The mouse shimmered palely in the candlelight.

'I'd been visiting a shrew in the garden and lost my way on my return journey. I have a cosy mouse hole in the skirting board of your father's study — at least, I did have . . .'

The mouse paused and let out another little sigh before changing the subject.

'You must be the daughter,' it said, looking up at Ada. 'The little Goth girl. The one that stomps around in those big boots.'

'That's right. My name's Ada,' said Ada politely. 'What's yours?'

'Call me Ishmael,' said the ghost of a mouse. 'Anyway, I was keeping to the shadows, head down, when I picked up this delicious scent wafting down the corridor towards me. Well, I couldn't resist. I followed my quivering nose and it led

THE BEIGE
CURATE

me to this lump of cheese — yellow with bluish bits and a smell like a stable boy's socks . . .'

Ishmael closed his eyes and his entire body flickered appreciatively.

'Sounds like Blue Gormly*,' said Ada. There were several truckles in the kitchen larder the last time Ada looked. Not that she went to the kitchen very often. It was run by Mrs Beat'em, who was very large and very loud and far scarier than any ghost. She spent her time inventing recipes and writing them down in an enormous book while shouting at her kitchen maids and making them cry. Her food was extremely complicated and often difficult to eat, needing twenty-three different knives, forks and spoons at breakfast and lunch. Even more cutlery was required at dinner. Her rhinoceros-foot jelly and baked sea-otter pie in a reduction of scullery maid's tears was Lord Goth's favourite dish, though Ada preferred

Foot Note.

*Blue Gormly is one of the lesser-known cheeses of England. Together with Somerset Stink, Mouldy Bishop and Cheddar not-so-Gorgeous, it is also considered one of the stinkiest. Personally I think it smells fine.

a soft-boiled egg and soldiers herself.

'Blue Gormly?' said Ishmael. 'It smelled delicious, whatever it was. I reached out to take it when . . . SNAP! Everything went black.' He gave a little shudder.

'The next thing I know, I'm white and see-through and hovering in the air looking down at myself caught in a horrible mouse-trap.'

MRS BEAT'EM

'How awful!' said Ada.

'I couldn't bear to look,' said Ishmael sadly, 'so I floated away and, I don't know why, but something drew me here, to your room . . .'

'Perhaps I can help,' said Ada, although she wasn't exactly sure what she could do.

Ishmael shrugged and said, 'I don't see how –' he paused – 'unless . . .'

'Unless what?' said Ada.

'Unless you came with me and collected the trap,' the ghost of a mouse said, his whiskers quivering. 'Before any more innocent mice get hurt.'

'That's a good idea,' said Ada.

Tiptoeing silently in her tightrope-walking slippers, Ada followed Ishmael as he led her out of her bedroom, down the corridor and through the long gallery towards the top of the grand staircase. Moonlight flooded through the tall windows, illuminating the portraits on the walls. There was no sign of the white nun, Ada noted, but the eyes of the portraits seemed to follow her as she tiptoed past.

There was the 1st Lord Goth, with a pudding-bowl haircut and a lacy ruff, and the 3rd Lord Goth, with a painted-on beauty spot. The 5th Lord Goth had a lopsided powdered wig and a big belly and seemed to be in a bad mood.

'This way,' said Ishmael, floating down the stairs.

Ada looked around. There was no sign of the beige curate, so she climbed on to the banister and slid to the foot of the staircase with a big *whoosh*.

At the bottom of the stairs Ishmael was waiting for her.

'The corridor was somewhere over there,' he said, pointing. Ada felt a flutter in the pit of her stomach.

'The broken wing!' she breathed.

Ada's home was enormous. There

THE 1ST LORD GOTH

THE 2ND LORD GOTH

THE 3RD LORD GOTH

THE 4TH LORD GOTH

THE 5TH LORD GOTH

was an east wing, a central hall with a magnificent dome, a west wing and, at the back of the house, the oldest part of Ghastly-Gorm, the broken wing.

It was called the broken wing because it was in need of repair. But it was out of sight and was such a jumble of overlooked rooms, abandoned bathrooms and neglected hallways that each Lord Goth had forgotten about it and concentrated instead on building new bits on to the other, more visible, parts of the house.

The 4th Lord Goth had added the dome and over four hundred ornamental chimneys, while the 5th Lord Goth had built the magnificent portico at the front of the house and the new kitchens in the east wing. Ada's father was the 6th Lord Goth, and he had concentrated on the west wing, adding drawing rooms and libraries and a stable block for his hobby horses. He had employed the finest landscape architect of the age, Metaphorical Smith, to lay out the gardens of Ghastly-Gorm Hall with many fashionable features, such as a

METAPHORICAL SMITH

rockery featuring a thousand Alpine gnomes, the overly ornamental fountain and a fashionable hobby-horse racecourse.

Ada and Ishmael made their way across the huge hall beneath the magnificent dome and through a small doorway half hidden by a thick tapestry. The corridors were long and dark and cobwebby, with dozens of doors lining the walls. Most of the rooms were empty, with peeling wallpaper and crumbling plaster ceilings, but a few were filled with old, forgotten things – the sorts of things Ada liked best.

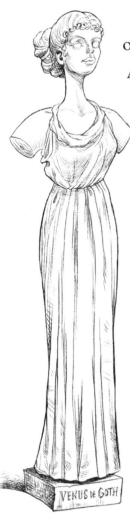

VENUS de GOTH

In one room there was a portrait of a lady with a haunting smile. Another room was full of vases decorated with pictures of Chinese dragons, and a third room housed a statue of a beautiful goddess with no arms.

Eventually Ishmael stopped and pointed at a pair of double doors with bronze hoops for handles.

'There!' he said excitedly.

Ada looked. In front of the doors was a mousetrap with a piece of Blue Gormly attached to it. Gently Ada nudged the mousetrap with the tip of a toe.

Snap!

The vicious trap sprang shut. Ada bent down and picked it up. Just then, from the other side of the doors, Ada heard a

familiar and unwelcome voice. 'Got another one!'
it wheezed.

The doors began to creak open, but not before
Ada had turned and bolted.

Chapter Two

Ada wasn't sure how long she had been running, but it seemed like an awfully long time.

When she finally stopped and looked around Ishmael was nowhere to be seen. She found herself in a small passageway that opened on to a courtyard and stepped out into the moonlight.

She was at the back of the house where the gardens were wild and untended. There were big curling brambles and briars, overgrown shrubs and bushes of enormous size. A small wooden sign read 'The Back of Beyond Garden (unfinished)'.

Ada had been meaning to explore this garden for ages but had been distracted by governess trouble.

Not that Ada got into trouble with the governesses, in fact she usually liked them, and tried to be as well behaved and helpful as she could.

No, it was the governesses themselves that were the problem.

They came from the 'Psychic Governess Agency of Clerkenwell' and seemed to arrive completely out of the blue, usually appearing a minute or two after Lord Goth had made a casual comment about Ada needing a proper education.

The first governess was Morag Macbee. She came from Scotland and had a single tooth and a large wart on the end of her nose of which she seemed very proud.

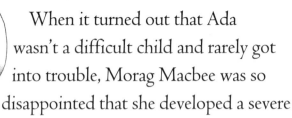

When it turned out that Ada wasn't a difficult child and rarely got into trouble, Morag Macbee was so disappointed that she developed a severe skin rash and had to go back to Inverness to recover.

Next was Hebe Poppins. She walked like a penguin and was always bursting into song. Ada liked her, but when Hebe discovered that Ada wasn't shy or unhappy she got bored and ran away with a chimney sweep.

Jane Ear was even more disappointing. Ada suspected early on that she wasn't really very interested in being a governess at all. Instead she spent all her time making cups of tea and knocking on Lord Goth's study door. Lord Goth had to send her away when she tried to burn down the west wing.

After that, Nanny Darling turned up. She was in fact a sheepdog who thought she was a human.

20

Nanny Darling kept barking at Ada because she was convinced that Ada was about to fly away to some place called Never-Ever Land. Lord Goth eventually gave her a mutton bone and she left.

Nana Darling

Becky Blunt was even worse.

She had had problems in her past, and when she tried to steal the silver Mrs Beat'em chased her from Ghastly-Gorm Hall and out of the grounds with a soup ladle.

Becky Blunt

Finally Marianne Delacroix had arrived one stormy night. She came from Paris and called herself a revolutionary.

Marianne Delacroix

Ada had learned a lot from her. She taught her several rousing songs in French, how to knit and how to construct a sturdy barricade. They were just working on an interesting woodwork project involving a contraption for slicing the heads off dolls when Marianne went out in a skimpy blouse one day, caught a terrible chill and had to leave.

Since then Lord Goth seemed to have forgotten all about Ada's education, which was just as well because Ada had had quite enough of governesses for the time being.

The full moon shone down on the Back of Beyond Garden (unfinished) and Ada made a mental note to come back and explore it properly in the daylight. Turning away, she was just about to take the path that led round to the front of the west wing and let herself in through the Byzantine windows of the Venetian terrace when she heard a piercing squawk.

Ada looked up.

Swooping down out of the night sky came an enormous white bird with a curved yellow beak and a sticking-plaster cross on its belly. It glided over Ada's head and landed on the roof of a tumbledown stone building half hidden by undergrowth. As Ada watched, the bird disappeared through a hole in the tiled roof.

'Well, I never!' said a little voice, and, looking

down, Ada saw that Ishmael had appeared at her feet.

'Unless I'm very much mistaken, that bird is an ocean-going albatross,' he said. 'And I should know,' he continued wistfully, 'because I used to be a seafaring mouse . . .'

'Really?' said Ada, intrigued.

'It's all in my memoirs,' said Ishmael, small and silvery in the moonlight. 'I had just finished writing them when –' his eyes fixed on the mousetrap Ada was still clutching – '*That* happened.'

Ada drew back her arm and flung the mousetrap as far as she could into the tangle of the Back of Beyond Garden (unfinished).

'Thank you,' said Ishmael. 'Now let's find out what an albatross is doing in the old icehouse.'

'That's the old icehouse?' said Ada.

The new icehouse was in the kitchen garden beside the west wing. Lord Goth had had it built to house the finest ice, which he had shipped from

Walden Pond* in New England. Mrs Beat'em used the ice in her leaning ice creams of Pisa and her penguin-tongue sorbet.

'Yes. My friend the shrew lives in a water butt next door,' said Ishmael. 'She enjoys the peace and quiet.'

Ada crept quietly as she could through the tall grass and cow parsley towards the old icehouse. When she got to the door, she found it ajar. Ishmael slipped inside and Ada followed.

It took a little while for Ada's eyes to adjust to the gloom.

When they did, she could see that the inside of the old icehouse was one enormous room with a sunken stone floor piled high with large blocks of ice, each one the size of a packing crate. Sitting on top of the highest stack of ice blocks was a huge figure in a sailcloth coat adorned with ship's rigging. On its head it wore the bicorn hat of a sea captain and strapped to its feet were two planks of wood from the deck of a ship, while on

*Walden Pond is in fact a very large lake in North America that is crowded with holiday cabins and lake houses belonging to poets, philosophers and thinkers who 'just want to get away from it all'.

its shoulder was perched the albatross.

The figure's face was deathly white, with blue veins criss-crossing its temples and cheeks and a line of stitches running across its forehead. Its eyes were yellow with blue rings around them and its lips and fingernails were black.

Lord Goth was always inviting strange and interesting visitors to stay at Ghastly-Gorm Hall and was so preoccupied with his poetry that he often forgot who he'd asked. Ada always tried to be as polite and welcoming as she could whenever she met one of Lord Goth's forgotten guests.

THE POLAR EXPLORER

She gave a little curtsy and said, 'Good evening, I hope you're having a comfortable stay. My name is Ada – very pleased to meet you.'

'The pleasure is all mine,' said the figure, taking off its bicorn hat, 'Allow me to introduce myself. I am the Monster of Mecklenburg, but my friends call me The Polar Explorer.'

'Water, water everywhere,' squawked the albatross, 'nor any drop to drink!'

'I don't think I've ever met a monster before,' said Ada, thinking about sitting down on a block of ice but deciding against it.

'I'm not at all surprised,' said the Polar Explorer. 'We're quite rare, you know. There's me, and my ex-girlfriend and . . . well, that's it really. You see, I was stitched together by a brilliant young

27

student at the University of Mecklenburg as part of his mad science project . . .'

Ada suspected he hadn't talked to anyone for quite some time.

'Water, water everywhere, nor any drop to drink!' squawked the albatross again.

The Polar Explorer ignored it.

'He made me from bits left on the battlefield of Baden-Baden-Württemberg-Baden. I have the legs of a trumpet major, the arms of a grenadier, the body of a brigadier and the head of a pioneer sergeant first class.' The Polar Explorer smoothed down his lank, lifeless hair and put his bicorn hat back on his head.

'Marinated for a month in a tub of glue I was, and then brought to life by a lightning storm.' He smiled, revealing seaweed-green teeth.

'Unfortunately, things didn't get off to a good start,' he continued, shaking his head. 'A butcher's dog ran off with my left foot and the student was absolutely furious. He was a bit of a perfectionist. Said he couldn't possibly hand me in to his professor like that and stormed off to class.

He was ashamed of me, you see . . .' The Polar Explorer looked suddenly sad and his yellow eyes filled with tears.

'When his professor asked, the student said that a dog ate his homework.'

'You poor thing,' said Ada, sympathetically.

'I learned my lesson though,' said the Polar Explorer, patting a wooden trunk. 'Now I always carry a spare.'

He looked down at the ground.

'Well, after that things went from bad to worse until finally I just had to get away from it all.' The Polar Explorer wiped his eyes and smiled at Ada. 'So I borrowed a ship and went to the North Pole. Lovely place – beautiful scenery. But not very many people to talk to—'

'Icebergs, icebergs everywhere, nor any drop to drink!' squawked the albatross.

'So how do you know my father, Lord Goth?' asked Ada, trying to stifle a yawn. The Polar Explorer was fascinating, but it was so late it was beginning to be early.

'Oh, I don't know Lord Goth personally,' admitted the Polar Explorer, 'But I do know Mary Shellfish, the distinguished lady novelist – a very good listener, just like you, Miss Goth.'

'Please, call me Ada,' said Ada.

'Well, Ada,' said the Polar Explorer, as he patted the albatross perched on his shoulder, 'Coleridge here found this copy of the *Literary Review* on a deserted sailing ship last month.'

THE LITERARY REVIEW

OR

THE ARTISTIC, CULTURAL, BIOGRAPHICAL AND HISTORICAL JOURNAL

AUGUST 1799   NUMB. LXXXII

MARY SHELLFISH

DISTINGUISHED LADY NOVELIST TO ATTEND

LORD GOTH'S GRAND COUNTRY-HOUSE PARTY

AND THERE, TO WIT, WITH OTHER EMINENT GUESTS TO TAKE PART IN

THE METAPHORICAL BICYCLE RACE

AN EVENT OVER HALF A MILE NAVIGATED ON THE SADDLES OF VARIOUS HOBBY HORSES

AND

THE INDOOR HUNT

CONDUCTED THROUGH THE DELAPIDATED QUARTERS OF THE BROKEN WING OF GHASTLY—GORM HALL AND NAVIGATED ON THE SELF—SAME HOBBY HORSES. AN EVENT WITNESSED BY THE GOOD FOLK OF THE NEIGHBOURING VILLAGE OF GORMLESS IN THE COUNTY OF GHASTLYSHIRE. ENGLAND. AND CELEBRATED THROUGHOUT THE LAND.

ALSO IN THIS ISSUE

RADICAL CARTOONIST MARTIN PUZZLEWIT'S LATEST SERIES OF SATIRICAL PRINTS ON THE LIFE AND TIMES OF THE LANDSCAPE ARCHITECT **METAPHORICAL SMITH**, ENTITLED

A GARDEN RAKE'S PROGRESS

PRINTED FOR TRISTRAM SHANDY GENTLEMAN AT THE DOLPHIN IN LITTLE BRITAIN, AND SOLD BY DR JENSEN IN WARWICK LANE; WHERE ADVERTISMENTS ARE TAKEN IN, AS ALSO BY FABERCROMBIE AND ITCH, RADICAL WEST LONDON WEAVERS OF PUTNEY

The Polar Explorer reached into his sailcloth cloak and pulled out a tattered journal. He pointed to the cover with a black-nailed finger.

'It says here that Mary Shellfish will be one of the guests at your father's grand house party and will be taking part in the Metaphorical bicycle race followed by the annual indoor hunt . . .' The Polar Explorer gave a green-toothed smile, 'and I thought I'd surprise her.'

Ada frowned.

She didn't look forward to Lord Goth's grand house parties. Each year, lords, ladies, poets, painters and deranged cartoonists arrived and turned Ghastly-Gorm Hall upside down. Mrs Beat'em got into an awful state preparing the banquet and Ada was expected to be heard and not seen more than ever. The bicycle race could be quite fun, but Ada never liked the indoor hunt, which involved the guests chasing small creatures through the broken wing with butterfly nets. Even though they released them outside afterwards,

Ada thought it was cruel. Unfortunately the indoor hunt was very popular, and each year the villagers of the little hamlet of Gormless marched up the drive holding flaming torches and gathered outside to watch it through the windows.

Just then the gong sounded in the kitchens of the west wing. It was four o'clock and the kitchen maids were getting up.

'I've got to go,' said Ada.

The Polar Explorer nodded and put a black-nailed finger to his black lips.

'Not a word,' he whispered with a wink.

Chapter Three

y the time Ada had run all the way round the west wing, in through the Byzantine windows, across the central hall, up the grand staircase, along the corridor and into her enormous bedroom she was exhausted. Climbing into her eight-poster bed, she drew the curtains, flopped back on to her giant pillow and fell into a deep sleep.

When she was awoken by the sound of the great-uncle clock chiming on her mantelpiece, Ada was startled to realize it was eleven o'clock already.

She jumped out of bed and rushed over to her dressing room. Pushing open the door, she stepped inside.

There, on the Dalmatian divan, were her Wednesday clothes – Scotch bonnet, Highland shawl and black tartan frock. Ada's clothes were chosen for her each day and evening by her lady's maid, Marylebone, who was so shy that Ada had never actually seen her. Marylebone had been Ada's mother's maid and before that she had been her mother's assistant, in charge of making all her tightrope-walking costumes.

That was just about all Ada knew about Marylebone, because she spent all her time hiding in the enormous closet in Ada's dressing room. But sometimes, if Ada didn't put on her clothes straight away, she'd hear a low growl coming from the depths of the closet.

Ada quickly got dressed and pulled on her big, clumpy boots before setting off for the short gallery, where each morning Mrs Beat'em's kitchen maids laid out breakfast on the sideboard.

She had got to the top of the grand staircase and was just contemplating whether or not to slide down the banister when she felt a hand on her shoulder.

'Why, if it isn't the young mistress herself,' said a thin, wheedling voice. 'Thought I heard you clumping down the corridor.'

Ada turned to see the tall, thin figure of Maltravers, the indoor gamekeeper, peering down at her.

He had pale grey eyes, long white hair and smoke-coloured clothes that seemed to match his skin. Ada didn't like to admit it, but she was a little bit afraid of him. Wherever Maltravers went, he carried a big bunch of keys, attached to his waistcoat by a long chain. They jingled when he walked and Ada could usually hear him coming, as long,

MALTRAVERS

that is, as she wasn't wearing her big, clumpy boots, which tended to drown out other sounds.

Maltravers smelled of wet carpets and mildew and had been the indoor gamekeeper at Ghastly-Gorm Hall for as long as anyone could remember. His job was to stop crows from roosting in the ornamental chimneys, hornets from building nests in the attics, ornamental Chinese deer from chewing the tapestries and blue-tailed newts from laying eggs in the bathtubs. He used nets, fumigating powders and traps of all shapes and sizes.

And when he wasn't busy netting, poisoning and trapping things, Maltravers spent his time in the broken wing, preparing animals for the annual indoor hunt.

One year it was sooty pigeons from Rochdale, another it was long-eared rabbits from the Isle of Wight, while for three years in a row it had been miniature drawing-room pheasants that Maltravers had hatched specially.

Once they were caught in big long-handled butterfly nets, the creatures were released into the grounds, where they often thrived. The three ornamental deer[*] from eight years ago had done so well that there were now at least a hundred in the dear-deer park.

Ada always thought Maltravers, who had a mean, unpleasant look on his face most of the time, seemed disappointed when the creatures were freed, and more than once she'd seen him looking at Lord Goth's blunderbuss longingly.

Ada shuddered.

'I saw someone creeping about in the broken wing last night,' said Maltravers, his pale grey eyes narrowing to slits. He gave a mirthless little laugh. 'Though I'm sure it couldn't have been the young mistress, could it?'

Ada could feel herself blushing and bit her lip.

'Because she wouldn't disappoint her father by

Foot Note

*Ornamental deer are extremely expensive, having to be smuggled out of China in the pockets of explorers and diplomats all the way from the Emperor's Palace in the Absolutely-Forbidden-I-Won't-Tell-You-Again City.

not wearing those fine clumpy boots he gave her, now would she?'

'Of course not,' said Ada, backing away.

'But just so you know,' he continued, his pale grey eyes now wide and unblinking, 'the broken wing is out of bounds until the annual hunt on Saturday night.'

Ada watched as Maltravers strode down the grand staircase, his keys jangling. He crossed the great hall to the small door behind the tapestry before disappearing through it.

'Out of bounds?' said Ada defiantly. 'We'll see about that.'

She clumped down the stairs and across the great hall, then through several smaller halls, each containing assorted marble sculptures of classical gods and goddesses, until she came to the short gallery.

Breakfast was waiting on the Jacobean sideboard*.

There was jugged hare, potted vole,

*The Jacobean sideboard is one of the ugliest pieces of furniture in the entire Hall, but due to its huge size and weight, and the fact that it is nailed to the floor, nobody is able to move it.

pigeon cooked
eight ways
and jellied
moorhen,
all on large
silver platters
beneath
gleaming silver
lids.

Ada ignored
them and helped herself to a soft-boiled egg and
four pieces of hot buttered toast that had been
cut into silhouettes of Prussian grenadiers. She
sat down at the table and was dipping a grenadier
into her egg when the yellow wallpaper opposite
rippled like the surface of a pond.

Ada dropped her toast in surprise.

A boy stepped away from the wall. He was the
exact same colour and pattern of the wallpaper he
has been standing against. If he hadn't moved, Ada
wouldn't have seen him at all.

'How do you do?' said Ada politely, 'I don't think we've met. I'm Lord Goth's daughter, Ada.'

The boy sat down at the table and changed colour to match the chair he was sitting on.

'I'm William Cabbage. My father, Dr Cabbage, is building a calculating machine for Lord Goth in the Chinese drawing room,' the boy explained. 'I hope I didn't startle you. I have a way of blending in with my surroundings. It's called chameleon syndrome.'

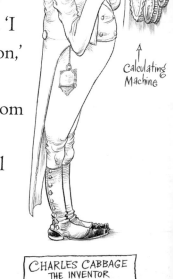

↑ Calculating Machine

Charles Cabbage was an inventor whom Lord Goth had invited to stay at Ghastly-Gorm Hall six months ago but then had forgotten about. 'I didn't realize Dr Cabbage had a son,' said Ada.

'And a daughter,' said a voice from behind her.

Ada turned round and saw a girl about her own age emerging from behind the sideboard.

CHARLES CABBAGE
THE INVENTOR

The girl had a wooden box strapped to her back, with a folding chair and a jar containing paint-brushes attached to it. Under one arm she carried a large portfolio, and on her feet she wore big, soft shoes.

'I'm William's sister, Emily,' she said. 'William! Please stop showing off and put some clothes on!' Emily told her brother.

outdoor
slippers

EMILY CABBAGE

William giggled, then got up from the table and crossed to the window, where he stepped behind the curtains.

'I didn't hear you come in,' said Ada, standing up.

'That's because I'm wearing outdoor slippers,' said Emily Cabbage. 'Father said we shouldn't bother you so we've been trying to stay out of your way. William has been blending in and I've been in the back garden painting in watercolours.' She frowned. 'Please don't tell him we bothered you. We didn't mean to. We thought you must have had breakfast ages ago, so we came in to have soft-boiled eggs and soldiers. Then we heard you clumping down the hallway in those big boots of yours . . .'

Ada smiled. 'I had rather a late night,' she said, and stepped forward and took Emily's hand, 'and you're not bothering me in the slightest.'

She looked down at her clumpy boots, then back at Emily. 'I only wear these because my father says I must. He believes children should be heard and not seen.'

William stepped out from behind the curtains. He was wearing a suit of blue corduroy with yellow socks and brown boots. Above his white collar, his face matched the curtains.

Ada led Emily over to the sideboard and took two soft-boiled eggs and a plateful of hot buttered grenadiers and handed them to Emily.

'I'd be delighted if you and your brother would join me for breakfast. Boiled egg and soldiers are my favourites.'

'Ours too,' said Emily.

They all sat down at the table together. William dripped egg yolk down the front of his jacket, but Emily's manners were extremely dainty. Ada was impressed.

When they had finished, Emily opened her portfolio and showed Ada her watercolours of plants and flowers she'd discovered in the Back of Beyond Garden (unfinished). Ada thought they were very good. William held up a watercolour of a purple briar rose and turned the exact same colour.

Ada laughed.

'I've told you once – stop showing off, William,' said Emily sternly. She smiled at Ada. 'You must forgive my little brother, Miss Goth. He sometimes takes his talent for blending in a little too far.'

Ringing
Seed
pod

Singing
Knot hole

E. Cabbage.

A Singing-ringing Tree

'Please, call me Ada,' said Ada warmly. 'It's so nice to talk to someone of my own age for a change. It can get quite lonely sometimes. The kitchen maids are too frightened of Mrs Beat'em to talk to me and the only other person I see is Maltravers the indoor gamekeeper and I'm a bit afraid of him. I don't like to bother my father because he seems so busy, though I do see him once a week in the long gallery for tea . . .'

Ada was aware she was talking rather a lot. But she liked Emily. She was talented and well-mannered and liked soft-boiled eggs with soldiers.

She wanted to tell William and Emily about Ishmael, and about the Polar Explorer hiding away in the old icehouse, but wasn't sure she should. Ada didn't want to frighten them. After all, Ishmael was a ghost and the Polar Explorer was a monster. Perhaps it would be wiser to wait until she was better acquainted with the Cabbage children.

'We don't find Ghastly-Gorm Hall lonely in

the least,' said William, turning stripy to match the teacup he was holding. 'We've made some very good friends in the Attic Club and they're all about our age.'

'Ssshhh! William!' said Emily crossly, 'The Attic Club's meant to be a secret!'

'I'm good at keeping secrets,' said Ada, intrigued. 'What is the Attic Club? If I promise not to say a word, can I join it?'

'Well,' said Emily, blushing pink behind her freckles, 'the Attic Club isn't meant for the likes of you, Miss Goth (I mean, Ada). It's a club for young servants and children of people who work for your father.' She looked down at the tips of her outdoor slippers.

'After all, you're the daughter of a lord. You have a fancy governess who came all the way from France to teach you and one day you'll be Lady Goth . . .'

'Miss Delacroix caught a chill and had to leave,' said Ada, reaching out and patting Emily's hand. 'But she did have some very interesting ideas about knitting and cutting the heads off dolls, which I'd love to share with you and your friends in the Attic Club, if you'll let me.'

'And you promise not to tell a soul about us?' said Emily, looking up.

'I promise,' said Ada.

Chapter Four

After their late breakfast, William went to the Chinese drawing room to help his father. At least, that's what he told Ada. Emily said the real reason was that he wanted to practise blending in with the Chinese dragon wallpaper. 'It keeps him happy for hours,' she said, rolling her eyes.

'Would you like to come painting with me?' she asked Ada. 'The Attic Club doesn't meet till after dark, so we've got plenty of time.'

'I'd love to,' said Ada.

She clumped back extra noisily to her bedroom so Lord Goth was bound to hear her, before taking off her boots and slipping on her black pumps. Then she took her sketching tablet and crayon box and tiptoed downstairs to meet Emily on the Venetian terrace.

'I love your slippers,' said Emily.

Together they made their way around the side of the west wing and along the path to the Back of Beyond Garden (unfinished). Ada peered into the thick tangle of briars, hawthorn saplings and towering banks of cow parsley. The roof of the old icehouse was just visible, but there was no sign of the albatross, or the Polar Explorer for that matter.

'Let's go this way,' said Ada, leading Emily away from the icehouse to be on the safe side.

They trampled down the long grass, doing their best to avoid stinging nettles and thorny brambles. After a little while Emily stopped, took the wooden box from her back and untied the small stool and water jar. She sat down with the box on her knees and, undoing the brass clasps, opened it. Inside there was a brass water bottle and a dazzling array of water colours with names like Naples Yellow, Alizarin Crimson, Hooker's Light Green and Payne's Grey.

Emily filled the jar with water from the brass water bottle and took a sheet of thick paper from her portfolio, then used the portfolio to lean on. Ada trampled down the grass, and sat down next to her.

'What are you going to paint?' she asked.

'That plant over there,' said Emily pointing with her paintbrush to a large shrub with yellow leaves and bright crimson flowers. 'It's a Mimsy Borogrove – beautiful specimen,' she observed.

'I'll draw a monster,' said Ada,

A MIMSY BOROGROVE

opening her crayon box. 'From my imagination,' she added quickly.

She drew a picture of the Polar Explorer in his big sailcloth cloak, with a white face and pale eyes and black lips and fingernails. She finished by drawing the albatross sitting on his shoulder in white chalk.

'You've got an excellent imagination,' said Emily. 'Imagine someone looking like that.'

'You're very talented,' said Ada, hastily changing the subject.

When Emily's painting had dried, she put it in her portfolio and packed everything up.

They were making their way back towards the house when Emily tripped on something in the undergrowth that sent her sprawling. Ada helped her back to her feet and then parted the long grass.

There, poking up from a half-hidden stretch of gravel, was one of Metaphorical Smith's little wooden signs. 'The Secret Garden Path', it read.

'The path is rather overgrown,' said Ada, 'but if you look really carefully, you can just make it out . . .'

'How exciting! Let's follow it!' said Emily.

They took it in turns to lead the way, ducking under low branches and jumping over tailing brambles, and following the path deeper and deeper into the Back of Beyond Garden (unfinished).

Eventually they came to a high wall with a small wooden door in it. On the door was a battered brass plate, with the words 'The Secret Garden' engraved on it. Ada pushed the door, which slowly swung open on squeaky, rusty hinges.

She took Emily's hand and they stepped inside.

The Secret Garden was a mess.

The grass was as tall as Ada and Emily. Weeds of every shape and size crowded in from the flower beds, and old, gnarled trees with twisting, curling branches reaching down to the ground competed with each other for space.

Ada and Emily followed the path, hand in hand. After a few maze-like twists and turns, they came to another wall, even higher than the first, with a wooden door that was even smaller.

On the door was another brass plate. This one read 'The Even-More-Secret Garden'.

Emily pushed at the door.

Then Ada pushed at the door.

Then they pushed at the door together, but it was no good: it wouldn't budge.

'How disappointing!' said Emily. 'I'd love to see inside.'

Ada stepped back and noticed a keyhole. 'It's locked,' she said. 'And I wouldn't be surprised if Maltravers has the key . . . Oh no, I almost forgot!' she suddenly exclaimed. 'It's Wednesday! Today is the day I take tea with my father in the long gallery! I'd better go back and change! We'll have to investigate this another time.'

Foot
Note

*The great-uncle clock on Ada's mantelpiece was a present to Lord Goth from his grand-father's brother. Little Ben, an amateur clock maker who trained mice to run up his clocks and wind them up.

'If you still want to join the Attic Club,' said Emily, when they got back to the Venetian terrace, 'meet William and me at the top of the grand staircase at ten o'clock tonight.'

'I'll see you there!' said Ada breathlessly, and dashed off in the direction of her dressing room. When she got there she found her Wednesday-evening clothes waiting for her. She put on the Hungarian frock and jacket and then changed her black pumps for the big, clumpy boots. The great-uncle clock* on the bedroom mantelpiece struck five.

'Mustn't be late,' Ada muttered to herself as she dashed out of her bedroom and down the corridor as noisily as possible. When she got to the entrance to the long gallery she stamped her feet extra hard.

'Come in, daughter,' said Lord Goth in a quiet yet elegant voice.

Ada marched into the room, her footsteps making the teacups rattle.

'Yes, yes,' said Lord Goth. 'You can stop stamping – I can see you now.' He avoided looking at her directly, she noticed. 'Come and pour the tea.'

Sitting in one of two wing chairs by a tall window, he was wearing riding boots and breeches and a pale blue tailcoat with silver fur collar and cuffs and one of the magnificent silk cravats that he had made fashionable; they were known as Gothkerchiefs in his honour. He put down the blunderbuss he had been idly polishing and crossed his legs.

Ada gave a little curtsy and noticed Lord Goth twitch uneasily when their eyes met.

He looked away and gazed up at the portraits on the wall opposite while Ada poured two cups of China tea from the silver teapot on the table. She handed one cup to her father and then, taking the other, sat down on the other chair.

For a while neither of them spoke. Ada didn't mind though. Lord Goth was the most famous poet in England and she was very proud that he was her father. She sipped her China tea.

Lord Goth looked out of the tall window at the rolling green grass of the dear-deer park beyond. In the distance, the extremely expensive herd of ornamental Chinese deer were grazing peacefully in the early-evening sun.

Next, Lord Goth placed his teacup on the table and gazed thoughtfully at the magnificent plaster ceiling of the long gallery.

'Maltravers tells me that his favourite trap is missing,' he said quietly and elegantly. 'I don't suppose you know anything about that?'

Ada stared into her teacup.

'I don't like Maltravers,' she said in a small
voice.

'Nobody likes Maltravers,' said Lord Goth,
'but he has been at the Hall for as long as anyone
can remember and besides . . .' he continued, still
avoiding Ada's glance, 'I need him for the indoor
hunt. So, no more creeping about outside the
Bathroom of Zeus.'

'The Bathroom of Zeus?' said Ada, her green
eyes sparkling. She was intrigued.

'In the broken wing,' said Lord Goth, turning at
long last to look at his daughter, 'It was built for
the 3rd Lady Goth. It is where Maltravers hatches
the miniature pheasants . . .'

Lord Goth paused and Ada saw a familiar look
of pain and sorrow cross her father's face.

He rose to his feet and, picking up the
blunderbuss, he turned to the tall window.

'Since Miss Delacroix left us, you've had too

much time on your hands, Ada,' he said quietly. 'I think it is high time we considered engaging another governess . . .'

Ada sighed and put her teacup down on the table.

'Now, if you'll excuse me,' said Lord Goth bleakly, 'I have a sudden need to shoot at gnomes.'

Ada left the long gallery and returned to her room, where she found her supper waiting for her.

She lifted the big silver lid covering the tray.

Underneath was a smellywich (two slices of bread with a piece of Blue Gormly between them), an apple from the kitchen garden and a glass of elderflower cordial.

'I bet that smells delicious,' said a little voice close by.

Ada looked down and saw Ishmael twinkling palely from the middle of the Anatolian carpet.

'But being a ghost, I don't seem to have a sense of smell, or an appetite for that matter,' he added sadly.

'Where did you disappear to?' she asked.

Ishmael shrugged. 'Oh, here and there,' he said vaguely. 'Though I always end up back here because, it seems, you're the only one who can see or hear me.' He paused and gave a small see-through shrug. 'For some reason I don't understand, I appear to be haunting you.'

'That's fine by me,' said Ada, who had developed an affection for Ishmael. 'You can haunt me for as long as you like if it'll make you feel better.'

The ghost of a mouse sighed. 'You're very kind,' he said mournfully.

While Ada sat on her chaise short and ate her

supper, Ishmael told her all about his life. He'd left home as a young mouse, escaped to sea and had all sorts of adventures.

'. . . Then I made very good friends with two parrots and a toucan . . .' Ishmael was saying when the great-uncle clock on the mantelpiece struck ten.

'Is that the time!' exclaimed Ada jumping up and rushing over to the foot of the eight poster bed where she hid her black leather pumps, 'I must be going. I'm meeting some friends in the attic. I don't suppose,' she said turning to Ishmael, 'you'd like to come with me?'

'I'd be delighted' said Ishmael, twinkling, 'and don't worry, I'll be as quiet as a mouse.'

Chapter Five

Ada tiptoed to the top of the grand staircase as quietly as she could, though it wasn't easy. The higher she went, the creakier the stairs became, until, as she approached the attic landing, every step caused a creak or a squeak.

'Very good,' said Emily Cabbage, who was waiting for her on the landing. 'I hardly heard you coming.'

Ada noticed that Emily was wearing her outdoor slippers. There was a ripple as William Cabbage stepped away from the plaster wall. 'Put your clothes on, William!' said Emily. There was another ripple as William stepped back into the shadows. He emerged a moment later in a flowing nightshirt.

'Follow me,' he said.

They walked along the attic corridor that ran the

length of the east wing past a row of closed doors. The sound of low, rumbling snores filled the air.

'The kitchen maids,' explained Emily, 'They go to bed at eight o'clock sharp because they have to get up so early.'

She stopped outside one of the doors and tapped on it lightly. The door opened and a small girl in a large cap and apron stepped out. When she saw Ada she looked startled, then blushed and gave a little curtsy.

'Ruby the outer-pantry maid, miss,' she mumbled.

Ada smiled and held out her hand.

'Please, call me Ada. Lovely to meet you. None of the maids have ever talked to me before,' she said as Ruby shyly shook her hand.

RUBY THE OUTER-PANTRY MAID

'That's because Mrs Beat'em says we're not allowed to,' Ruby said.

She glanced at William and Emily and her bottom lip trembled. 'I won't get into trouble, will I?'

'What happens in the Attic Club stays in the Attic Club,' said Emily firmly.

They continued down the corridor and turned the corner into a dark passageway at the end of which was a ladder fixed to the wall. At the top of the ladder was a trapdoor. Emily climbed the ladder and pushed open the trapdoor. She looked down at Ada, who was staring up at her.

'Welcome to the Attic Club,' she said with a smile.

Ada climbed the ladder, followed by Ruby and William. Stepping through the trapdoor, she found herself in a huge room with a sloping ceiling consisting of hundred of criss-crossing struts and beams. Along one side, close to the ground, were small round windows through which shafts of moonlight shone down across the dusty floorboards. In the centre of the attic was a table made of fruit crates, ringed by old coal sacks stuffed with dried haricot beans, some of which had spilled out on to the floor. Two boys, both a little older than William, were sitting on the sacks. When they saw Ada, they jumped to their feet.

'Don't be nervous,' said William. 'Ada has come to join the Attic Club. This is Kingsley, the chimney caretaker, and this is Arthur Halford the hobby-horse groom.'

Ada had seen the hobby horse grooms in the grounds of Ghastly-Gorm Hall, but, like the kitchen maids, they never talked to her.

Arthur Halford was short, with wire spectacles and unruly fair hair. He wore an oil-stained smock with various tools attached to it and a Gothkerchief knotted at his neck.

ARTHUR HALFORD THE HOBBY-HORSE GROOM

By contrast, Kingsley the chimney caretaker was tall and thin, with spiky black hair and a pair of brushes strapped to his back like two sooty wings. He wore leather knee pads and black boots that were even bigger and clumpier than Ada's.

'I used to be the chimney caretaker's apprentice but then Van Dyke the chimney caretaker ran away with your governess, Hebe Poppins, so I got promoted,' said Kingsley with a smile.

'And I look after your father's hobby horse, Pegasus,' said Arthur, not wanting to be outdone. 'I'm getting it ready for the metaphorical bicycle race.'

KINGSLEY THE CHIMNEY CARETAKER

William, Emily and Ruby each sat down on a coal sack while Kingsley and Arthur shared one so that Ada could take the remaining seat.

'I declare this meeting of the Attic Club open,' said Emily, rapping on the table with the wooden spoon Ruby had just handed her. 'Who would like to go first?'

Arthur and Kingsley both reached for the wooden spoon in Emily's hand, but William beat them to it.

Holding up the spoon, he blended in with the blue-grey shadows behind him. 'I've been doing some very interesting blending-in recently,' he said, 'in the oldest part of the house.'

'The broken wing!' exclaimed Ada excitedly.

Emily took the spoon from her brother and handed it to Ada.

'Only the person with the spoon is allowed to speak,' she told her.

Ada took the spoon.

'The broken wing,' she repeated a little more calmly before handing the spoon back to William.

'Yes,' said William. 'Two days ago I followed that gamekeeper Maltravers. He was collecting mice from his traps and then resetting the traps with cheese . . .'

From close by Ada heard Ishmael let out a little gasp, but nobody else seemed to notice. Looking down, she saw his outline shimmering at her feet.

'He opened a pair of doors with brass handles and crept inside,' William went on. 'He was definitely up to something. But he closed

the doors before I had a chance
to take a look.'

Ada took the spoon again.
'That room is called the
Bathroom of Zeus, and it is where
Maltravers hatches the miniature
pheasants for my father's indoor
hunt,' she told them.

Ruby reached out and
gently took the spoon from
Ada with an apologetic smile.

'Mrs Beat'em says she's fed up
with Maltravers and his strange
demands,' she reported. 'First it
was Blue Gormly for his traps, and
then it was porridge oats, a whole
sackful, and then three smoked
salmon, not to mention most
of the carrots from the
kitchen garden.'

Emily held out her hand

and Ruby gave her the spoon.

'Whatever he's keeping in there has certainly got an interesting appetite,' she said. 'Porridge, smoked salmon, carrots and dead mice . . .'

Ada heard a strangulated sob ending in a squeak.

'I propose that the Attic Club find out what Maltravers is keeping in the Bathroom of Zeus,' Emily concluded, looking round the table.

'If you ask me,' said Ada, taking the spoon, 'Maltravers is up to no good.'

The rest of the meeting was taken up by reports from other members. Kingsley the chimney caretaker was a talented climber and had discovered some ornate chimneys* on the east wing that he wanted the rest of them to see. Arthur Halford, meanwhile, was a talented mechanic, and had perfected a safety harness they could wear while they did so.

Ruby, a talented cook, reported that she was getting everything they would need for

*The ornamental chimneys of Ghastly-Gorm Hall are some of the finest in the land. 'The Barley Sugar', 'The Hedgehog' and 'The Six Chimneys of Henry VIII' are among the more ornate examples.

a rooftop midnight feast, and William told them that he would borrow his father's telescope so they could all stargaze.

Ada didn't say anything. Every member of the Attic Club had a special talent, it seemed, except her. 'What can I do?' she asked.

'You have a wonderful imagination,' said Emily, squeezing her hand. 'I'm sure you'll think of something.'

At eleven o'clock Emily placed the wooden spoon on the fruit-crate table and they all went off to bed.

'When's the next meeting?' whispered Ada as she parted from William and Emily on the stairs.

'Same time next week,' said Emily.

'But the indoor hunt is on Saturday night!' said Ada. 'That's only three days away!'

'Don't worry, we can talk about our Maltravers investigation at breakfast tomorrow,' said Emily reassuringly.

Ada said goodnight and crept back to her room.

Glowing faintly in the dark, Ishmael followed her.

Ada found her nightgown laid out on the Dalmatian divan and got changed for bed. Then, yawning sleepily, she climbed into the eight-poster bed, blew out her candle and drew the curtains before falling straight to sleep.

'What a strange day it has been,' said Ishmael with a little sigh.

Chapter Six

Ada sat up in bed and peered into the inky blackness, suddenly woken by the sound of carriage wheels crunching on the gravel outside. She lit her candle and tiptoed across her enormous bedroom to the window.

On the driveway in front of the steps leading to the magnificent portico of Ghastly-Gorm Hall was a black carriage drawn by four black horses with curling black feathers on their black bridles. Slowly the door to the carriage opened and a woman stepped out. She wore a black dress and jacket, black gloves and shoes, a broad-brimmed black hat and a heavy veil. In one hand she carried a large black carpet bag decorated with a skull pattern, and in the other a black umbrella. Ada stepped back from the window as the woman walked soundlessly up the step. Moments later she heard a sharp *rat-tat-tat* as the woman knocked on the front door.

The carriage wheels crunched on the gravel once more as the black carriage, which didn't seem to have a driver, disappeared into the night. Below, Ada heard the front door creak slowly open and Maltravers's wheezing voice say, 'Yes?'

'Miss Borgia from the Psychic Governess Agency,' said a beautiful lilting voice with the hint of a foreign accent.

'Come in,' said Maltravers stiffly. 'You'll find the governess quarters in the dome. Lord Goth doesn't like to be disturbed.'

'I know,' said Miss Borgia softly, 'That is why I am here. The agency specializes in the education of inconvenient children.'

'Inconvenient is right,' muttered Maltravers. 'And don't let her fool you with her clumpy boots and polite manners,' he went on, and Ada shivered at the sound of his voice. 'She's a sneaky one, that little Goth girl.'

The next thing Ada knew, the great-uncle clock on the mantelpiece was striking nine.

She yawned and stretched, then jumped out of bed.

In her dressing room she found her Thursday clothes – a Venetian taffeta dress, an Ottoman coat with pompoms and a red tasselled hat. Ada got dressed and was about to put on her big, clumpy boots when she paused.

Then she turned and walked back into her enormous bedroom and over to the eight-poster bed, where she put her black pumps on instead.

She crossed to the door, opened it and peeked out. There was no sign of the governess and no sign of Maltravers. Ada tiptoed out of her bedroom and down the corridor as quietly as she could.

When she reached the short gallery Emily and William Cabbage were waiting for her at the Jacobean sideboard.

'Venison sausages in onion custard or porridge-crusted kippers in strawberry gravy?' said William lifting several large silver lids and turning brown, then yellow, then strawberry.

'Soft-boiled egg and soldiers,' said Ada.

'Delicious!' said Emily, when they had finished. 'You know, it's Ruby's job to cut the toast. She chooses a different regiment each morning.'

Just then, William, who was sitting by the curtains and had taken on a floral pattern, dropped his toast and pointed out of the window.

'Look!' he said. 'There goes the indoor gamekeeper.'

Ada and Emily looked.

Maltravers was striding along the gravel path outside Ghastly-Gorm Hall.

'What is the *indoor* gamekeeper doing *outside*?' asked Emily.

'Going to his room, probably,' said Ada. 'When he isn't working, Maltravers lives in the garden.'

'Let's follow him,' said William.

They made their way quickly down the grand staircase and turned into the east wing. They ran past the Egyptian drawing room, the pre-Columbian drawing room and the Chinese drawing room, where Charles Cabbage was

hard at work inventing. They continued, passing
several more drawing rooms whose furniture had
been covered by dust sheets for as long as Ada
could remember, before reaching the kitchens.

In the inner pantry the inner-pantry maids
were dusting jars, labelling preserves and filling
boxes with fresh ice from the new icehouse. None
of them looked up or even seemed to notice as
William, Emily and Ada dashed past.

In the parlour several tearful parlourmaids were
sorting through wooden spoons, arranging them
in pots according to size, and were also too busy
to notice.

In the big kitchen beyond, Mrs Beat'em sat in a
huge rocking chair beside a gigantic kitchen range.
She was furiously scribbling in a big battered book
whose pages were feathered with little notes stuck
on with flour-and-water paste. She was wearing
an enormous cap that dwarfed her furious red
face and an apron the size of a large tablecloth.
From her belt were slung pastry nozzles, meat

tenderizers, egg whisks and rolling pins of every size and design, which clinked and clattered as she rocked.

'Agnes, fuddle those eggs!' Mrs Beat'em roared like an enraged sea lion, 'Maud, bedevil the batter! No, not that batter, you idiot! Pansy, frizzle those pies until they're piping hot, then frangellate the crusts – quickly, girl!'

Weeping kitchen maids jostled and elbowed each other as they worked at the range or round the three kitchen tables, which were laden with bowls and baking trays and measuring jugs.

'Come on!' said William. 'We mustn't let him get away!'

Ada and Emily hurried after William as he crossed the kitchen and entered the outer pantry. This was a small room with an extremely high ceiling. The walls were lined with cupboards and shelves, all full of spices, herbs, flour, sugar, tinctures and extracts in tiny bottles. From the ceiling hung bundles of parsley, sage, rosemary and thyme together with three soup trumpets, a pastry trombone and several flutes for freezing sorbets.

Sitting on a high stool at a desk Ruby the outer-pantry maid was patiently making seahorses out of radish shavings to decorate Mrs Beat'em's Neptune broth. When she saw Ada she blushed.

'Hello, Miss G . . . Ada,' she said.

'We're following Maltravers,' Ada whispered. 'By the way, I love those seahorses. You're very clever.'

Ruby blushed again.

'Nelly! Neptunize those prawns, NOW!' Mrs Beat'em's voice screamed in the big kitchen.

Ada, William and Emily ran out of the outer pantry and into the kitchen garden beyond.

'Careful!' whispered William, pulling Ada and Emily behind a stand of runner beans and turning green. 'There he goes now.'

Maltravers had rounded the corner of the new icehouse and was striding through the flower beds of the bedroom garden beyond. Reaching the Sensible Folly*, Maltravers took a key from the bundle attached to his waistcoat, unlocked the front door and went inside.

Ada, Emily and William crept through the bedroom garden and approached the building. Crouching down, they peeked in at one of the carefully glazed Grecian windows. Maltravers was sitting at the desk with an envelope in his hand.

As Ada, Emily and William watched, the indoor gamekeeper opened the envelope with a paper knife and read the letter inside before pinning it to the wall with a paper fork. Then he reached into the envelope and took out a folded banknote. He carefully unfolded it and held it up to the light. Printed on its very fine paper

Foot
Note

*The Sensible Folly was built by Metaphorical Smith to look like a ruin of a Grecian Temple but had a good roof, decent guttering and excellent plumbing while, next to it, the Lake of Extremely Coy Carp was really just a lake that Metaphorical Smith had forgotten to stock with goldfish.

in swirling letters were the words 'The Bank of Bavaria promises to pay the bearer of this note five pounds'.

William whistled softly. He had turned the colour of white marble.

'That's a lot of money!' he whispered.

Maltravers got up and walked over to the bed. He reached underneath it and pulled out a metal box which he unlocked. Inside were more banknotes. Maltravers placed the five-pound note on top of the other notes and locked the box before sliding it back underneath the bed. With a low, wheezing laugh he lay down on the bed and closed his eyes.

My Dear Sir, I have great expectations of Lord Goth's house party and trust your preparations are complete. Enclosed is the final payment. Hansel and Gretel are looking forward to their big night!

Yours in Anticipation,

Rupert von Hellsung

CRETAN
REVIEW OF BOOKS

C R E T E

Isle of sun sea sand and literature

A D V E R T I S E M E N T S

Mr OMALOS the faun is pleased to announce a special event for one week only – weather permitting

A SLIM VOLUME
OF POETRY
BOOK TASTING

Delicious volumes of verse, undusted, leatherbound to the most delicious standards

THE HIBERNIAN
SHOWJUMPING
GAZETTE

Shetland **C**entaur Hamish jumps a clean round in the Shetland Pony Trials on the island of Jura. Among other contestants Shaggy the brave hoof and Jock the goat also jumped exceptionally well and were a close second and third. Attendance however was rather disappointing, with the crowd consisting of mostly puffins and a few disgruntled crofters.

A Minotaur from Egg won the first caber-tossing championship ever attempted in Edinburgh during the Literary Festival

FABERCROMBIE
and
ITCH

INTELLECTUAL WEAVERS OF WEST LONDON

REQUEST ATTENDANCE AT A

PUBLIC MEETING

TO SOLICIT OPINIONS and seek assistance in the matter of

clothing the GREAT APES OF THE BATAVIAN JUNGLE

recently rescued from the cruelties of

VAN DER HUM·S TRAVELLING MENAGERIE

— Namely —

THE WILDMAN OF PUTNEY
and
THE WIFE OF BARNES

The Ancient and Modern Mariners'
JOURNAL

WATER WATER EVERYWHERE NOR ANY DROP TO DRINK

THE ITHACA OPEN-AIR OPERA'S PRODUCTION OF
THE ODYSSEY

Featuring Siren Sesta and the Harpies

Tos et ius, secaepratas aritios siminimendam eium esequi ulpa inimetust, tem quia quia volores serumque parupta simintatior aut doloresUr aditiis itationse pero voluptatur sum et in praturi tiatia doluptum rolloruntem custion sequae asi consed que earumquat omnibillaut aceperum nus aut voluptiam audi sit iam et qui ut haribus alic tota sed mo ma nis modist, caeda con con repudae rferore pelignam consed et odia con parcur iscius alignim agnatestem qoe ne vendia ipid quam estrumqui berum fuga. Nem. At latisimiliae nobiscim fuga. Nequam res se offit tem antis ium fuga. Nequam con perum nobit ad moluptat volumqui ut dolorro invelen dandianisAd quistis de nis molorem. Oriidele simusto eum endi quiat porpos dolorporro il in re iminus quis endis aut odis ante veruptatquae ni vella quis renditi ostium quas et alique is dolor ma ate voluptati apicimi liquantis nobit, vendemquiam ratendis et et re nonsedit, coribus dolupta eptatur sa illa sandaeptatur sollatur? Quishcia eatempor aut volorempor sum simagnimi, sequae vel et volorum fuga. Nam qui et voluptatem uta ducit quatquam quatus a dis rolut voluptaquam quidemp erepuda ndiciat quasim inci voieneota vel impore, qui omnis expelit Veremporumque porro mintium voloritas enimenducim volo doio magnam quia dem. Iliquamet omniandit, in num rest ut exerum nimil ipiciis aecullu dignimo eliquis et asere

Ada shivered as she saw the thin, unpleasant smile on his face.

William pressed his nose up against the glass of the window and narrowed his eyes as he peered at a letter pinned to the wall above the desk.

'My dear sir,' he read, 'I have great expectations of Lord Goth's house party and trust your preparations are complete. Enclosed is the final payment. Hansel and Gretel are looking forward to their big night! Yours in anticipation, Rupert von Hellsung.'

'What is Maltravers up to?' he muttered. 'What preparations? And who are Hansel and Gretel?'

'They sound pretty grim,' said Emily, shaking her head.

'One thing is certain,' said Ada. 'Maltravers is up to no good!'

On the truckle bed the indoor gamekeeper seemed to be snoring.

'You wait here,' Emily told William, 'in case he

wakes up. Ada and I are going to the Bathroom
of Zeus – to find out what he's keeping in
there. It may have something to do with these
"preparations".'

Chapter Seven

Ada led Emily across the hall to the tapestry and pulled it aside, to reveal the small doorway to the broken wing.

'Follow me,' she said.

They went down a flight of stone stairs and along a dark corridor with doors lining the walls.

Ada paused and opened one of the doors. Emily and Ada peered inside. The room was empty, except for an old wardrobe containing some moth-eaten fur coats. Ada closed the door and shook her head.

'I was sure the Bathroom of Zeus was around here somewhere . . .' she said.

Just then, from further down the hallway, there came the sound of singing. It was soft and soothing and very, very beautiful.

Ada and Emily followed the sound. It was

coming from behind a pair of double doors with brass hoops for handles.

'The Bathroom of Zeus!' Ada whispered excitedly.

Emily took one hoop, and Ada took the other, and they pulled. As Emily and Ada stepped through the gap and looked around, the singing stopped.

In the centre of the room was a sunken pool full of stagnant green water, in the middle of which stuck up a rock with a nest of twigs and branches on top. And sitting on the nest was one of the strangest creatures Ada had ever seen.

THE SIREN SESTA

With the head of a woman and the body of a large bird, this was certainly not a miniature drawing-room pheasant.

The bird woman looked up. Her eyes were the colour of a wine-dark sea, while her hair was cormorant black, the dark curls swept back and held in place by a headdress of shimmering bronze.

Her body was covered in feathers the colour of dark seaweed, while her tail and wings were a bright gold and matched the glittering talons on her feet.

Ada couldn't take her eyes off the creature. Of all the strange, forgotten things she had encountered in the rooms of the broken wing, this had to be the strangest and most beautiful.

Beside her she heard a clatter and a clink as Emily slipped her watercolour box from her shoulders and unhitched her camping stool and water jar.

'Hello,' said Ada, as clearly and politely as she could manage. 'My name is Ada and I'm very pleased to meet you.'

The bird woman tilted her head to one side like a curious seagull and Ada could see a row of needle-sharp teeth glinting when she spoke.

'I is Sesta the Siren,' she said in a musical voice, 'star of the Ithaca Open-Air Opera House . . . it's more of a rock in the sea actually,' she added with a twinkling laugh. 'But still, the sailors is come from all over to hear me sing.'

'What are you doing here?' asked Ada.

Emily had got a piece of watercolour paper out of her portfolio and had started painting, her eyes wide with wonder.

'The famous Lord Goth!' the Siren Sesta exclaimed. 'He invite me his self. Me and my backing singers, Orphia, Eurydice and Persephone . . .'

ORPHIA, EURYDICE &
PERSEPHONE THE HARPIES

Ada had been so mesmerized by the sight of the bird woman, she hadn't noticed the birdcage hanging from the ceiling above her head. It contained, she now saw, three more bird women who were much smaller than the Siren Sesta and had large eyes and sharp, pointy noses.

'Is very nice to meet you,' they chorused, flapping and fidgeting on their perch.

'See, here . . .' The Siren Sesta rummaged in the nest beneath her and grasped a thick gilt-edged but slightly grubby card in her talons, which she held up for Ada to read.

To *Miss Siren Sesta and the Harpies*
Lord Goth requests the honour of your attendance at
A Country-House Party
AT
Ghastly-Gorm Hall
GHASTLYSHIRE · ENGLAND
ON THE OCCASION OF
THE ANNUAL METAPHORICAL BICYCLE
RACE
&
INDOOR HUNT

'But what I not understand,' said the Siren, ruffling her feathers and shaking her foot, 'is when we come here, Lord Goth's man does this to me – look!'

Ada looked.

There was a manacle around Siren Sesta's leg with a chain that was attached to a heavy loop which in turn was bolted to the side of the pool.

The harpies rattled the bars of their cage, and Ada saw that there was a sturdy padlock holding the cage door shut.

'Lord Goth's man, he feed me smoky fish and to the girls, dead mouses.' The Siren's dark eyes flashed and she spread her golden wings wide. 'But we are artists – we cannot live like this!' Her beautiful voice echoed round the room.

'Like this, like this, like this . . .' the harpies harmonized from the cage above. Siren Sesta's gaze fell on Emily Cabbage and her watercolours.

'You're very beautiful,' said Emily appreciatively, mixing a seaweed green that matched Sesta's feathers.

The Siren stood still as statue as she looked down at Emily. 'I see you too have the soul of an artist,' she cooed. 'You must capture my beauty . . . and my suffering.'

Ada looked at the lock on the manacle around Sesta's leg.

'I'm so sorry, there must have been some sort of misunderstanding,' she said, 'I will tell my father, Lord Goth.'

But Ada knew that this wasn't a misunderstanding. Maltravers had invited the Siren and the Harpies to Ghastly-Gorm Hall and imprisoned them, and she had a nasty feeling that she knew why . . .

She looked around the Bathroom of Zeus. There wasn't a miniature pheasant to be seen, and the indoor hunt was set for the night after tomorrow, Saturday night.

'You are Lord Goth's daughter?' said Sesta, still holding her pose, 'I like you. You are very polite, I think. Not like Lord Goth's man . . .'

Just then
William Cabbage
came running
through the gap
in the doors. He
was the colour of
shadows and cobwebs
but changed to a
dusty marble
as he caught
his breath.
Pushing the
doors closed, he turned to Emily and Ada.

'Maltravers!' he gasped, hastily pulling off his jacket and unbuttoning his shirt. 'He woke up . . . He's coming this . . . way!'

Emily hastily packed up her watercolours, pulled her paintbox on to her back and tipped her painty water into the pool. She looked at Ada, then back at William.

'It's all right for you, William,' she said wildly.

'You can blend in, but there's nowhere for Ada and me to hide.'

Ada looked around. Emily was right. She could hear Maltravers's footsteps in the corridor outside as he approached the Bathroom of Zeus.

'Ada, Emily! Over here!'

Ada looked across the room to the fireplace on the far wall.

Kingsley the chimney caretaker's sooty face had just appeared, upside down, peeking out from below the mantelpiece.

'Here, take a hand each!'

Ada and Emily rushed over to the fireplace and grabbed Kingsley's outstretched hands.

'Take us up!'

Kingsley was hanging by his ankles from some sort of pulley contraption. Suddenly Ada felt herself being pulled up the chimney with impressive speed, as ancient, sooty brickwork whizzed past the tip of her nose in a blur.

Moments later they shot out into daylight and came to a halt. Ada and Emily let go of Kingsley's hands and stepped down from the ornamental chimney pot from which they had just emerged. Over the chimney was a wooden tripod with a rope and pulley attached, together with a weight and a lever which Arthur Halford was holding. He reached out and undid the straps attached to Kingsley's big, clumpy boots, and the chimney caretaker jumped down from the chimney pot to join them.

'This is an invention of mine,' said Arthur proudly. 'It's a dumb sweeper – a bit like a dumb waiter but for chimneys.'

'A little bit newfangled for my liking,' said Kingsley, not wanting to be outdone, 'but good

for getting out of scrapes in a hurry.' He smiled and Ada blushed.

'William told us to be ready in case you needed help' said Arthur. 'Members of the Attic Club stick together.'

'Thank you, Arthur,' said Emily, dusting soot off her portfolio, 'Maltravers almost caught us. What a nasty man he is!

And you won't BELIEVE who we just met. The strangest creature, but really quite beautiful . . .'

'Talking of strange creatures,' said Arthur, 'I made an interesting discovery in the old tumble-down buildings behind the hobby-horse stables this morning. You'd better see for yourselves.'

Arthur and Kingsley packed up the dumb sweeper, and then Kingsley led them over the jumble of rooftops of the broken wing. He pointed out the most interesting ornamental chimneys as they clambered over tiles, tiptoed along roof ridges and trotted down gullies and gutters. Eventually they came to a flying buttress with stone steps that led down to the ground.

'Take care,' Kingsley said, smiling at Ada, who felt herself blushing. He turned and trotted off over the rooftops as sure-footed as a mountain goat.

Ada held Emily's hand as they descended the stone steps and followed Arthur towards the back of the west wing.

As they got nearer, Ada could see the hobby-horse stables, a long, low building made up of a series of workshops with half-open stable doors. Inside each workshop, grooms dressed in smocks like Arthur's were hard at work, hunched over forges heating spokes and hammering out kinks in wheel rims, or standing at woodworking benches sanding curved beech chassis. On the walls, beside tools in racks, hanging on padded hooks, were the hobby horses themselves.

'I look after that one,' said Arthur, pointing to a splendid bicycle with a carved winged horse on its chassis. 'Its Lord Goth's favourite hobby horse.' They continued past the stables until they came to a series of small sheds with half-collapsed slate-tiled roofs and walls propped up by wooden stakes and scaffolding.

'These are the unstable stables,' said Arthur. 'Very few people come here any more.'

Foot
Note

*Shetland
centaurs are
just one of
a number
of mythical
creatures living
in Scotland.
The Glasgow
cyclops and
the Edinburgh
gorgon are well
known, but
the Arbroath
smokie, a
fire-breathing
mermaid, is
more elusive.

Emily and Ada kept close behind Arthur as he opened a rickety door and stepped into the dark, shadowy interior. It took Ada a little while for her eyes to adjust to the gloom. When they did, she gave a little gasp of surprise.

Chained to the wall by their ankles were two figures, one huge and one tiny. Both were extraordinary looking.

'This is Hamish,' said Arthur, 'He's a centaur from Shetland*.'

The centaur gave a little snort and pawed the ground with his hoof.

'And this is Mr Omalos, a mountain faun from the island of Crete.'

The faun put down the slim volume of poetry he had been nibbling and pulled at the sleeves of his shabby green velvet jacket.

HAMISH THE SHETLAND CENTAUR

MR OMALOS THE FAUN

'This is Ada, Lord Goth's daughter,' said Arthur, 'and her friend Emily Cabbage.'

Emily had already set up her watercolour box and was sketching excitedly.

Arthur turned to the faun. 'Tell them what you told me this morning.'

'Well,' said Mr Omalos in a deep, gruff voice that nevertheless had a kindly tone to it, 'I'm just a lowly faun – half-goat, half-book collector. I have a taste for old books, the dustier the better, but I only nibble round the margins, never the words themselves; the ink can be a little bitter . . .'

'What my friend is trying to tell you,' interrupted the Shetland centaur with a little whinny, 'is that your father, Lord Goth, invited us here for a country house party. We had invitations addressed to each of us personally, but someone I won't name ate them after we got here . . .'

'Sorry,' said Mr Omalos, looking sheepish as well as goat-like.

'Anyway,' snorted Hamish, 'that gamekeeper of

his showed us to these stables and then chained us up while we were sleeping. It's not on, I tell you. It might be a wee bit wild and windy in my paddock back home, but at least I have the run of the place!'

The little centaur kicked out with his back legs, tugging at the chain, before folding his arms and glaring at Ada.

'I'm very sorry,' said Ada. 'Lord Goth invites all sorts of guests to his country-house parties and sometimes things get a little confusing . . .'

She didn't want to frighten these poor creatures by mentioning her suspicions about Maltravers and the indoor hunt.

The centaur snorted, 'The porridge oats aren't bad,' he conceded.

'And the carrots are delicious,' added the faun, 'though perhaps a little too fresh for my taste . . .'

When Emily had finished her watercolours, she and Ada walked back towards the house. Arthur had left earlier because the metaphorical bicycle race and indoor hunt were only two days away and he had lots to do.

'You must tell your father what Maltravers is up to,' said Emily as they approached the Venetian terrace.

'I will . . .' said Ada, with a thoughtful frown. She turned to her friend, 'Have you got any more paper in your portfolio?' Emily nodded.

'Then there's something we need to do first.' Ada said.

Chapter Eight

'How good are you at climbing trees?' Ada asked Emily. They were standing outside the door to the Even-More-Secret Garden.

'Quite good,' said Emily uncertainly.

'Climbing trees is one of my favourite things,' said Ada. 'I think I inherited a sense of balance and a head for heights from my mother. She was a tightrope walker from Thessalonika.' Ada opened her locket and showed Emily the miniature painting inside.

'You look just like her!' Emily exclaimed.

Ada smiled, then closed the locket and pointed to a tree beside the high wall. 'This tree is perfect,' she said. 'Just follow me and copy everything I do.'

'I'll try,' said Emily.

She had taken off her watercolour box and put down her portfolio, to make it easier to climb, but

she had a pencil behind one ear and a folded sheet of paper in her pocket.

Ada climbed up the tree, finding hand- and foot-holds as she went. Emily followed gingerly. Up in the branches, Ada selected one that reached over the wall into the Even-More-Secret Garden and crawled along it.

Emily inched along behind her, until the branch spread out into lots of smaller branches with large green leaves and spiky horse chestnuts.

'Spreading chestnut trees are the most fun to climb,' Ada told Emily, who was holding on tight and trying not to look down. Ada parted the leaves in front of them.

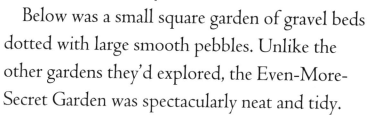

'Look!' she said.

'I can't!' said Emily.

Below was a small square garden of gravel beds dotted with large smooth pebbles. Unlike the other gardens they'd explored, the Even-More-Secret Garden was spectacularly neat and tidy.

At the centre of the garden was an elegant building of wrought iron and glass with a small wooden sign beside it that read 'The Greenhouse of Harmony'. Looking down from the overhanging branch, Ada could see through the glass roof. Inside the greenhouse were large pots containing strange plants with colourful leaves and exotic fruit hanging down in clusters.

Ada saw something else, and gasped. It was as she'd suspected.

'I don't think I've got your head for heights,' said Emily, turning green.

'Can I borrow your pencil and paper then?' asked Ada.

THE
GREENHOUSE
OF HARMONY

'If you can reach them,' said Emily, 'I'd rather not let go of this branch.'

Ada took the pencil from behind Emily's ear and the paper from her pocket and unfolded it. Then she turned her attention back to the Greenhouse of Harmony and the two figures she had spotted sitting inside.

They were great apes, with dark brown faces and beautiful orange-brown fur. Both were neatly and fashionably dressed. Ada sketched both of them carefully and was just folding the paper up to put back in Emily's pocket when she heard a key rattling in a lock. She stayed very still as, below, the door to the Even-More-Secret Garden opened and Maltravers entered, pushing a wooden wheelbarrow. Approaching the greenhouse, he took his keys and unlocked the glass door.

'The Wildman of Putney and the Wife of Barnes,' Maltravers said, in his thin, wheedling voice, 'just look at you! Those west-London intellectual weavers who rescued you certainly have excellent taste in clothes. They should fetch a pretty penny at the Gormless market.'

He reached out and took the Wildman of Putney's top hat, trying it on for size before dropping it into the wheelbarrow.

'I'm sure you weren't this well dressed when the intellectual weavers found you in that travelling circus.' He untied the Wife of Barnes's bonnet and pulled the shawl from her shoulders. She looked up at him with sad but kindly eyes.

THE WILD MAN OF PUTNEY

'I'm surprised the weavers let you come.'
Maltravers laughed unpleasantly as he took the
rest of their clothes and piled
them in the wheelbarrow.
'But then a personal
invitation from the
famous Lord Goth is very
persuasive, I find.'

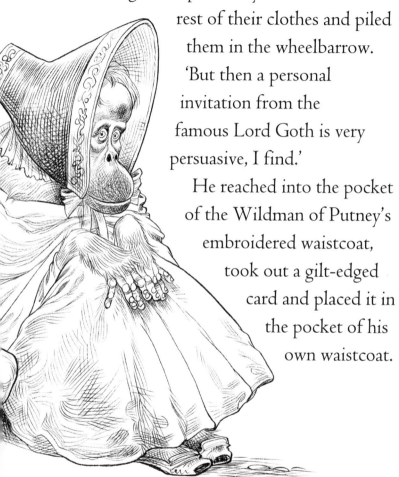

He reached into the pocket
of the Wildman of Putney's
embroidered waistcoat,
took out a gilt-edged
card and placed it in
the pocket of his
own waistcoat.

THE WIFE OF BARNES

Then the indoor gamekeeper wheeled the
barrow out of the greenhouse and locked the
door behind him.

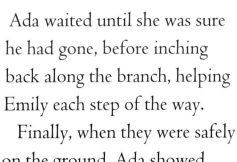

Ada waited until she was sure
he had gone, before inching
back along the branch, helping
Emily each step of the way.

Finally, when they were safely
on the ground, Ada showed
Emily her drawing. 'I suspected
that Maltravers had something
locked up in the Even-More-
Secret Garden,' Ada said
triumphantly. 'And if I'm right,
he's planning to use these poor
creatures in the indoor hunt on
Saturday.'

'That's very good, considering
you were up a tree,' said
Emily, putting the drawing
in her portfolio with her

watercolour paintings, 'but now you must go and tell your father about this terrible situation.'

When they got back to the Venetian terrace they found William by the Byzantine windows. He was the colour of white stucco plaster as he stepped away from the wall.

'I've been following Maltravers all day,' he told them, 'blending in and trying to get hold of those keys of his, but they're chained to his waistcoat, which he never takes off. I followed him to the kitchen garden, where he pulled up carrots, and then all the way to a secret walled garden. Funny thing is, he went in with an empty wheelbarrow and came out with it full of clothes . . . When I left him he was pulling up floorboards in one of the empty rooms in the broken wing . . . What on earth is he up to?'

'Put on some clothes,' said Emily, rolling her eyes, 'and we'll tell you.'

Just then there was a loud bang from across the lawn.

Ada and the others turned to see Lord Goth speeding past the rockery in the distance. He was riding his hobby horse Pegasus and had a smoking blunderbuss in his hand. Behind him several of the Alpine gnomes perched high on the rocks had lost their heads. Lord Goth gained speed as he rounded the corner of the rockery and sped along the front of the west wing towards the steps to the portico, gravel flying up from the spinning wheels. Reaching the steps, he dismounted and threw the hobby horse aside.

'If I'm quick I can catch him at his study door!' Ada exclaimed as she dashed into the house. 'See you tomorrow at breakfast!' she called over her shoulder.

Ada ran up the west staircase, along the first corridor and around the corner where the 1st Lord Goth's three-piece suit of armour* stood. There, coming from the opposite direction, up the grand staircase, was her father. Ada stopped when she saw the expression on Lord Goth's face. It was a mixture of shock and surprise and sadness as he looked into her eyes. Then his gaze travelled from her face down to her slippered feet, and his expression darkened.

'Father!' Ada began, 'I'm so sorry to disturb you like this but I've got to tell you about—'

'Ada,' Lord Goth

*The three-piece suit of armour was specially made for the 1st Lord Goth by his blacksmith and features a single body piece and two helmets, both of which are decoys to prevent the wearer getting his head cut off.

interrupted her in his quiet but elegant voice, 'you have disappointed me.'

'But, Father,' Ada protested, 'Maltravers—'

'Ada!' Lord Goth interrupted her again, his voice even quieter and more elegant. 'It is one of my closely held beliefs that children should be heard and not seen.'

'I know, Father, but—' Ada began.

'And yet I didn't hear you because you are not wearing the boots I gave you!'

'I know, Father, I'm sorry. I forgot—'

'Forgot?' echoed Lord Goth, striding past Ada and grasping the doorknob to his study. 'Forgot? Do my wishes mean so little to you? Next you'll be telling me you've been up on the rooftops.'

Ada's cheeks coloured and

she stared down at her black leather pumps. Lord Goth avoided looking at her as he pushed his study door open and stepped inside.

'Whatever you have to say to me,' he said as a quiet and elegant parting shot, 'you can say to me over tea in the long gallery the week after next.'

The door to his study clicked shut. Ada turned and walked slowly back down the corridor towards her own room. Next week would be too late. The indoor hunt was the day after tomorrow, on Saturday night. She thought about the poor creatures that Maltravers had tricked into coming – the Siren Sesta and the harpies, Mr Omalos and Hamish, the Wildman and his wife – all of them locked up by the indoor gamekeeper, and all of them about to be chased through the rooms of the broken wing by Lord Goth's country-house guests.

She thought of Maltravers in his room in the Sensible Folly, the five-pound note in the strongbox under the truckle bed and the letter pinned to the wall . . .

'. . . Hansel and Gretel are looking forward to their big night! Yours in anticipation, Rupert von Hellsung.'

Ada shivered. Hansel and Gretel? Whatever Maltravers was planning, it didn't sound like a normal indoor hunt.

She reached the grand staircase and was about to cross the landing and go to her room when a dark shape soundlessly descended the banister.

'Miss Goth,' said a soft-toned voice with the hint of a foreign accent, 'so we meet at last.'

Chapter Nine

da looked up. The dark shape stepped lightly off the banister and on to the landing.

Ada's new governess held out a white hand which Ada shook. It felt ice cold.

'Pleased to meet you,' said Ada.

'You can call me Lucy,' said the governess. 'I'd like us to be friends.'

Ada smiled uncertainly and wondered how long this particular governess would stay at Ghastly-Gorm Hall.

LUCY BORGIA

'Come up to the schoolroom,' said Lucy, 'and we can get acquainted.'

'Isn't it a little late?' asked Ada. The sun was setting and the shadows were lengthening outside.

'It's never too late to get acquainted,' said Lucy in a lilting voice. She climbed back on to the banister and held out an ice-cold hand to Ada.

'Besides, when you get to know me, you'll realize that I'm more of a night person.'

Ada took Lucy's hand and climbed up on to the banister next to her. Lucy tapped the banister with the sharp-tipped black umbrella she was carrying in her other hand and they began to slide upwards.

'How did you do that?' asked Ada, astonished, as they got to the top of the grand staircase.

'It's an old governess trick,' said Lucy, with a smile that reminded Ada of an old painting she'd once seen. 'And I'm a very old governess.'

'You are?' said Ada, intrigued.

THE MONA LUCY

They got down from the banister and entered the schoolroom.

'Yes,' said Lucy, 'I'm over three hundred years old.'

The school room was in the dome of Ghastly-Gorm Hall and was big and circular with an opening in the middle. The ceiling was covered in pictures of fat babies with wings, plump ladies in flowing robes and an angry-looking man who appeared to be chasing a swan. On one side of the dome was Ada's school desk and on the opposite side was the desk of the governess. They both faced the wall, but sound carried so well there that all one of them had to do was whisper and the other could hear her perfectly.

Ada followed Lucy through a small door and up

the stone steps of a spiral staircase. Opening the door at the top, Lucy was about to usher Ada inside when a startled looking ornamental deer darted out of the room and clip-clopped down the stairs.

'Come in, Ada,' said Lucy. 'Please, sit down.'

Ada sat on a low chair by the dressing table. On the dressing table was a mirror covered by a black handkerchief, a hatpin and what looked like a glass of blood.

Lucy sat down on the bed. At her feet was the large black carpet bag that Ada had seen her carrying the night before.

'Perhaps I'd better explain,' said Lucy.

Outside, a pale white moon had risen above Ghastly-Gorm

Hall, bathing the rooftops in a silvery light.

'You see, I am a vampire.'

Ada nodded even though she wasn't quite sure what a vampire was.

'I was once an Italian princess in the beautiful hill town of Cortona. I spent a lot of my time sitting on a balcony with a needle and thread, mending tights while young men played lute and sang to me from the courtyard below.

'Every so often one of the young men would try to climb up to the balcony and would ladder his tights, and I would feel obliged to mend them for him.'

Lucy smiled and a faraway look came into her eyes as she gazed out of the window at the full moon.

'Happy days,' she said softly.

Then she frowned, 'One day, a handsome Hungarian count came to visit my father. He brought with him a strange instrument that he played with a horsehair bow and which made a noise like a sobbing cat. I must admit I was caught off guard by this dashing nobleman.

'So one moonlit night, very much like this one, I let Count Vlad the fiddler climb up to my balcony after he had played to me. I was young and foolish and he wore chainmail leggings that protected his tights, so I let him take me in his arms.

'It was a fatal mistake. You see, he was a vampire* and, instead of kissing me, he bit me on the neck and turned me into a vampire like himself.'

'Did it hurt?' said Ada, wide-eyed.

'No, not really,' said Lucy. 'Just sort of

*Vampires are notoriously difficult to kill – a stake through the heart will turn a vampire to dust, a sharpened stick through the heart will turn him to pebble-sized rubble, while a really sharp pencil through the heart will turn him to recyclable cardboard.

tickled, although I think that was mainly his moustache . . . Anyway I was so cross I pushed him off the balcony and he landed on a wooden rose trellis below and crumbled to dust. Like a stake through the heart but more decorative.' She smiled ruefully.

'Well, I soon found out how awkward it is being a vampire – staying out of daylight, only drinking blood, wearing black all the time . . .'

'Black suits you,' said Ada. Being a vampire didn't sound like much fun, she thought, but Lucy Borgia seemed quite matter-of-fact about it.

'Thank you,' said Lucy. 'But after what happened to me I wouldn't dream of drinking human blood, so I feed on animals mostly and the occasional flightless bird. I don't harm them, of course,' she added, then pointed to the glass on the dressing table. 'Would you mind?'

'Not at all,' said Ada, passing the glass to the governess.

Lucy took a sip and closed her eyes.

'Ornamental deer's blood – delicious!' she put the glass back down and kicked off her slippers. 'So I took a gap century – a hundred years or so of wandering around trying to think of something to do. Finally I decided that what I really wanted to do was teach. So I became a governess. A duelling governess, to be precise.'

'A duelling governess?' said Ada, who thought this sounded even more exciting than being a three-hundred-year-old vampire.

'Here, I'll show you,' said Lucy, jumping lightly to her feet and opening her carpet bag.

Inside were rows of velvet trays which folded out on silver hinges, like the inside of a jewellery box. Cushioned on the velvet was a glittering array of beautiful umbrella tips. Lucy reached over and picked up her umbrella. She turned it over in her hand, expertly unscrewed the tip and selected a replacement. She twisted the new tip into place with a flick of her wrist and held the umbrella up.

'Sterling silver,' she said, 'perfect for duelling with a werewolf.'

She twirled the umbrella skilfully and replaced the tip with another.

'Polished bronze,' she told Ada, 'ideal for fencing with a minotaur.'

The umbrella whirred in her hand again.

'Ancient amethyst — just the thing for crossing swords with a

mummified pharaoh, and my personal favourite . . .'

She selected a long thin spike from a velvet tray and fixed it to the end of her umbrella.

'. . . polished driftwood for deterring a sabre-rattling vampire pirate.'

Lucy sprang back and forth on tiptoe, the umbrella held out before her in one outstretched hand, the other on her hip.

'With the right umbrella,' she told Ada, 'you can fight off any threat, confront any danger and . . .' she flicked the handle and the umbrella opened, 'stay dry at the same time!'

Ada's eyes sparkled as she looked at the umbrella and the velvet trays.

'I don't suppose,' she said, 'you've got anything for dealing with an indoor gamekeeper?'

Chapter Ten

It felt good to talk to Lucy Borgia and tell her all about Maltravers, and when at last Ada slid down the banister and tiptoed back to her room she was feeling much happier.

Climbing into bed, Ada was just about to blow out the candle when she heard a familiar little sigh. Ishmael, the ghost of a mouse, was standing in the middle of the Anatolian carpet twinkling palely in the candle light.

'It isn't much fun,' he said sadly, 'drifting about aimlessly, appearing and disappearing in the middle of the night like this . . . I don't seem to have any control over my own movements.'

'You poor thing,' said Ada sympathetically.

She realized guiltily that she hadn't thought about Ishmael all day.

He shook his head, 'I was a mouse of action, you see. I'm just not suited to being a ghost, floating and haunting, appearing and disappearing . . .'

Ishmael floated over to the eight-poster bed and looked up at Ada.

'This evening, when I appeared, the sun was just going down and the sunset was so beautiful I just wanted to float off into it and go towards the light . . .'

'Why didn't you?' asked Ada. She hated to see Ishmael so sad.

He shrugged. 'I don't know,' he said. 'I just couldn't. It's as if something was holding me back . . . keeping me here . . .'

'Why don't you tell me one of your tales?' said Ada. She was pleased to see Ishmael brighten and become less transparent.

'Well, I could tell you about my voyage to the

land of the Lilliputbugs . . .' he began.

Ada lay back against her gigantic pillow and closed her eyes.

When she woke, a thin shaft of sunlight was shining through a chink in the curtains and the great-uncle clock on the mantelpiece was chiming half past eight. Ada climbed out of bed and went into her dressing room. Her Friday clothes were a Somerset bonnet, a Wessex shawl and a Norfolk frock with an embroidered meadow-flower hem. Ada was careful to put on her big clumpy boots to please her father. Then she went to the short gallery to meet Emily and William for breakfast.

'There aren't any soft boiled eggs or soldiers,' said William looking at the embroidered flowers on Ada's frock. 'Ruby says Mrs Beat'em has got everyone working on the grand dinner this evening.'

'That's just what I want to tell you about,' said Ada, ignoring the three trays of rolled herring in marmalade sauce. 'My new governess . . .'

'You've got a new governess?' exclaimed Emily. Her face fell. 'Does that mean you won't be able to spend time with us now?'

'That's just it,' said Ada, taking Emily's hand and squeezing it. 'Lucy Borgia is a night person — our lessons will be after dark — so we can still sketch and explore during the day.'

'Did you tell your father about Maltravers and those poor creatures?' asked Emily.

'I tried but he wouldn't listen,' said Ada. 'Tonight is Friday, and the guests for the bicycle race and indoor hunt will be arriving this afternoon. But it's going to be all right,' she continued brightly, 'because Lucy promised that she would speak to him herself, at the grand dinner tonight. She said that what Maltravers has done is cruel and dishonest and that she isn't the least bit afraid of him. Lucy Borgia is a duelling governess, you know.'

'A duelling governess!' said William, turning cornflower-blue. He sounded impressed. 'What's a duelling governess?'

So, over breakfast of cold lettuce toast, Ada told William and Emily all about Lucy Borgia.

When she had finished, Emily closed the portfolio. She'd been looking through the watercolours of the creatures she'd painted as Ada talked.

'Well, I must say, that is quite a relief,' she said. 'I don't think a beautiful creature like a Siren should be used in an indoor hunt, even if she is released afterwards,' she went on. 'And that goes for the other creatures as well.'

'That's just what Lucy said,' Ada told Emily.

The Wildman of Putney   The Wife of Barnes

with Thanks to Ada
E. Cabbage.

Mr Omalos

E. Cabbage.

Siren Sesta

The Harpies

E. Cabbage.

Hamish

E. Cabbage.

'And I'm sure my father will listen to her, because she's a grown-up.'

'Three hundred years old,' said William, turning the exact same green as his half-eaten toast.

'Will you come to the Attic Club and show us what she teaches you?' he asked, his eyes lighting up. 'Umbrella fencing sounds fascinating, and very practical if it rains . . .'

Their minds at rest, the children spent the day playing carpet bowls in the long gallery and skittles on the Venetian terrace, painting landscapes in the dear-deer park and sailing paper boats in the overly ornamental fountain*.

Most of all, they avoided places where they might have run into Maltravers. Ada didn't want to give the indoor gamekeeper any warning before the grand dinner that night. She was sure Lord Goth would be very angry when he found out that Maltravers hadn't been hatching miniature drawing-room

Foot Note.

*The overly ornate fountain started as a simple horse trough but got added to by visiting sculptors, each trying to outdo the others. Finally they were made to stop when their creations took up so much space there was hardly any room for the water.

pheasants for the indoor hunt all this time. Instead he had been up to no good, and William had given Ada the evidence to prove it . . .

My Dear Sir, I have great expectations of Lord Goth's house party and trust your preparations are complete. Enclosed is the final payment. Hänsel and Gretel are looking forward to their big night!

Yours in anticipation,

Rupert Von Hellsung

FABERCROMBIE and ITCH

INTELLECTUAL WEAVERS OF WEST LONDON
REQUEST ATTENDANCE AT A

PUBLIC MEETING

TO SOLICIT OPINIONS and seek assistance in the matter of clothing the GREAT APES OF THE BATAVIAN JUNGLE recently rescued from the cruelties of

VAN DER HUM'S TRAVELLING MENAGERIE

Namely

WILDMAN OF PUTNEY and THE WIFE OF BARNES

THE HIBERNIAN SHOWJUMPING
GAZETTE

Shetland Scentaur Hamish jumps a clean round in the Shetland Pony Trials on the island of Jura. Among other contestants Shaggy the brave hoof and Jock the goat also jumped exceptionally well and were a close second an Attendance however was disappointing, with the consisting of mostly puffin few disgruntled crofters.

A Minotaur from won the first championship ever attemp Edinburgh during the literari

RETAN
EVIEW OF BOOKS

C R E T E

of sun sea sand and literature

VERTISEMENTS

r OMALOS the faun is pleased to announce a ecial event for one week ly - weather permitting

SLIM VOLUME OF POETRY
BOOK TASTING

elicious volumes of verse, ndusted, leatherbound to he most delicious standards

The Ancient and Modern Mariners' JOURNAL

WATER WATER EVERYWHERE NOR ANY DROP TO DRINK

THE ITHACA OPEN-AIR OPERA'S PRODUCTION OF THE ODYSSEY

Featuring Siren Sesta and the Harpies

'Maltravers has gone to a lot of trouble,' said William, as his paper boat sank in the overly ornamental fountain for the third time, 'He must have wanted this year's indoor hunt to be extra special.'

'Probably just showing off,' said Emily, dipping her water jar in the water.

'I'm not so sure,' said Ada, thinking of those five-pound notes, 'But the important thing is that Lucy Borgia's going to tell my father and he'll put a stop to it,' she said firmly. 'After all, if word got out that the guests of Ghastly-Gorm Hall were being chained up and imprisoned, then nobody would come to his country house parties ever again.'

Just then there was the sound of carriage wheels scrunching on gravel, and Ada, Emily and William looked up to see a line of grand carriages coming through the gates and approaching the house down the drive.

'Speaking of guests,' said William, turning the colour of a ridiculously rococo stone mermaid — that is to say, very pale, 'here they come now.'

The carriages swept past the overly ornate fountain and drew up in front of the portico steps. The front door of Ghastly-Gorm Hall opened and Lord Goth stepped out, followed by Maltravers.

In the first carriage, an elegant four-seater, was Lady George, the Duchess of Devon, and her companion Tristram Shandygentleman. They were Lord Goth's oldest friends and came to his house party every year.

Lord Goth greeted them warmly and

LADY GEORGE, THE DUCHESS OF DEVON

TRISTRAM SHANDYGENTLEM

ushered them inside together with the three portly Dalmatians that had been riding with them in their carriage.

The next vehicle, a scruffy-looking buggy with holes in the roof, contained the party poets, Molebridge and O'Quincy. They argued with each other all the time but they never missed a country house party.

Lord Goth shook them both by the hand, only for the poets to get into a heated discussion about who should go after whom through the door.

Behind the party poets' carriage was an open-topped cart pulled by two shire horses. It contained

THE POETS
MOLEBRIDGE & O'QUINCY

Dr Jensen, the cleverest man in England, and his biographer, MacDuff.

Ada had never heard Dr Jensen say a word. He wore dark spectacles and enormous tartan trousers. MacDuff was extremely skinny and did all the talking. He carried a long-handled club with him at all times because of his morbid fear of red squirrels.

With great effort Dr Jensen climbed down out of the cart and brushed straw from his enormous trousers before silently shaking Lord Goth's hand. MacDuff followed, telling Lord Goth something very clever

DR JENSEN & MACDUFF

Dr Jensen had just said to him. When they had gone inside Lord Goth came down the steps to greet the occupant of the next carriage.

This was a single-seater donkey trap belonging to Martin Puzzlewit, the radical cartoonist.

He had white hair and a frown and always wore boxing gloves, even when he was drawing, so that he'd always be ready for a fight.

Fortunately this was seldom necessary because no one could ever understand his cartoons well enough to take offence. Lord Goth tried to shake hands but found it impossible, so patted the radical cartoonist on the back instead before turning to the last carriage, which had just drawn up.

MARTIN PUZZLEWIT, THE RADICAL CARTOONIST

This was a magnificent coach of Bavarian pine, with a pair of stag's antlers mounted at the front and back. It was pulled by a team of six prancing Austrian show ponies in crimson livery. The door to the coach opened and a set of crimson velvet steps descended to the ground. A slender arm reached out, and Lord Goth gallantly took the black-gloved hand that appeared before him and kissed it. There was a girlish giggle from inside the coach and a slim, elegant young woman stepped out. She was dressed in a black jacket with a lace ruff-collar and a black striped skirt.

'Mary Shellfish, lady novelist,' she said, 'I'm delighted to make your acquaintance, Lord Goth – I'm a great admirer of your poetry.'

Lord Goth let go of Mary Shellfish's hand and gave a small bow.

MARY
SHELLFISH,
THE LADY
NOVELIST

'The pleasure is all mine,' he said in a quiet yet elegant voice. Mary Shellfish held up a leather-bound book in a black-gloved hand.

'This is a copy of my bestselling novel,' she simpered, 'entitled *The Monster, or, Prometheus Misbehaves*. Perhaps you've heard of it.'

But before Lord Goth could reply a great white seabird swooped down from the sky. Snatching the book from Mary Shellfish's hand, the seabird flew off with it in its long yellow beak and disappeared over the rooftops.

'You told me your novel was popular,' said a deep voice from the depths of the coach, 'but this is ridiculous.'

Moments later a tall figure in a broad-brimmed hat and a black bearskin cape emerged from the coach. He had blue eyes the colour of ice, a long thin moustache that was waxed to needle points at its ends and a large jaw that jutted out when he spoke.

Mary Shellfish blushed and gave a girlish giggle.

'This is Rupert von Hellsung,' she told Lord Goth. 'My carriage broke a spoke a few miles back and Herr von Hellsung rescued me by the roadside. Imagine my surprise and delight when we discovered that we were both your guests, Lord Goth.'

Lord Goth raised an eyebrow and Ada could tell that he didn't remember inviting a Rupert von Hellsung to his country house party but was too polite to say so.

Behind him, Maltravers stepped forward.

'I believe Herr von Hellsung is the hobby-horse champion of Munich, my lord,' he said in his thin, wheedling voice.

'Indeed?' said Lord Goth, with an elegant smile. 'Welcome to Ghastly-Gorm Hall,' he said, shaking Rupert von Hellsung's hand. 'Dinner is at eight.'

RUPERT VON HELLSUNG

Chapter Eleven

da clumped up the stairs and along the corridor to her room. She hoped her father could hear her, because she had hated disappointing him by not wearing the big, clumpy boots the day before. But everything was going to be all right, she told herself as she pushed open her bedroom door. Lucy Borgia would see to that. Ada had only known her for one day, but already she was beginning to think she might be the best governess she'd ever had.

Dinner was at eight and Ada knew that she would be expected to sit quietly at the end of the steam-engine dining table and listen to the brilliant conversation of Lord Goth's distinguished guests. None of the guests ever talked to Ada though, because she was just a child and couldn't possibly have anything interesting to say, and besides, they were too busy thinking up brilliant things to say themselves. Ada wished that Emily and William had been invited to the grand dinner.

Ada went into her dressing room and found her Friday-evening clothes laid out on the Dalmatian divan. There was a satin gown of midnight blue, a pair of black elbow-length gloves embroidered with stars and a crescent-moon tiara with a swan-feather clasp.

Ada put on the gown and gloves and then pinned up her hair and put on the tiara. She looked down. On the floor next to the divan, instead of her big clumpy boots, there was a pair of elegant black slippers with clicketty-clack heels.

Ada smiled.

On special occasions Ada was allowed to wear less noisy shoes, and the grand dinner before the metaphorical bicycle race and indoor hunt was a special occasion.

Ada put on the slippers and did a little twirl

in front of the big looking glass. An appreciative
growl came from the depths of the closet.

Ada gave a little curtsy and went down to
dinner.

The dining room of Ghastly-Gorm Hall was
in the east wing. It had tall windows with fine
views over the dear-deer park along one side.
Along the other wall was an indoor viaduct,
which led from a Corinthian serving hatch
by the door to the long dining-room table in
the centre of the room and back again.

A model railway track led out of the
serving hatch, along the viaduct and around
the table. The track came from the kitchens
of Ghastly-Gorm Hall, and a small steam
engine called the Gravy Rocket* ran along it.
On special occasions this was used to carry
Mrs Beat'em's dishes up to the guests, who
could help themselves to whatever caught
their fancy as the steam engine chugged
slowly passed. After completing a circuit of

*The Gravy
Rocket is a
miniature
version of the
famous steam
engine the
Salad Rocket,
which was used
to transport
carrots and
cabbages from
Norfolk to
London until
it crashed into
the Mayonnaise
Express just
outside the
little town of
Coleslaw.

the table the Gravy Rocket would trundle back to the kitchens to be refilled by the waiting kitchen maids, ready for the next course.

When Ada got to the dining room, the Gravy Rocket's whistle could be heard in the kitchen and Lord Goth's guests were taking their places at the table. Ada sat down at her place at the end.

Dr Jensen was throwing bread rolls at Martin Puzzlewit, who was angrily knocking them away with his boxing gloves. At the head of the table

Lord Goth smiled quietly and elegantly and pulled the bell rope beside his chair. A few moments later the steam engine, which had been designed and built for Lord Goth by the son

of an engineer called Stephenson, came chugging
through the Corinthian serving hatch by the door
and along the indoor viaduct.

As Ada watched, Stephenson's son's Gravy
Rocket rounded a bend and wobbled past her
on to the dining-room table. Everyone served
themselves as it went past.

The steam engine trundled back on to the
viaduct and headed towards the Corinthian serving
hatch. The sounds of chugging and rattling faded
briefly into the distance
before growing louder
again. With a tooting
whistle the Gravy
Rocket re-emerged from
the hatch and
rattled towards
the table, its
carriages
refilled with
steaming dishes.

As it rolled by, Dr Jensen threw a rhubarb and duck flan at Martin Puzzlewit, which hit him on the forehead.

'As Dr Jensen says, when a man's tired of rhubarb, he's tired of life . . .' said MacDuff as the cartoonist shook his gloved fist at him.

'I might not be good at drawing hands, but I can draw really big noses!' Puzzlewit raged. 'You just wait and see . . .'

Ada sank down in her seat. This was a typical dinner, with food fights and arguments and nobody listening to anyone else.

She looked out through one of the tall windows. The sun had set and the full moon was shining down on the dear-deer park. The ornamental Chinese deer cast moon shadows in the silvery light.

Ada looked over her shoulder at the door to the dining room.

Where was Lucy Borgia? she thought anxiously.

Lord Goth was sitting back in his chair with a bored expression on his face as the Duchess of Devon told a story about one of her overweight Dalmatian hounds using her carriage to chase cats. The steam engine rattled past and headed back to the kitchen.

Just then, the door opened and Lucy Borgia entered the room.

Dr Jensen was flicking spoonfuls of apple-and-bacon trifle at Martin Puzzlewit, who was swinging at him with his boxing gloves while MacDuff told Mary Shellfish and Tristram Shandygentleman what Dr Jensen had said about lobsters.

None of the guests paid any attention to the white-faced woman dressed in black as she strode up to Lord Goth. Stopping by his chair, she tapped him lightly on the shoulder with her umbrella.

At that moment, the Gravy Rocket returned fully laden from the kitchen. It steamed along the indoor viaduct and set off across the table.

Ada sat up in her chair.

'Lord Goth, there is something I must tell you . . .' Lucy Borgia said in a clear voice.

At that moment Martin Puzzlewit swung his fist at Dr Jensen on the other side of the table and hit a carriage carrying a generous pile of snails steamed in their shells and a large sauce boat. The snails went everywhere, while the sauce boat flew through the air, spattering the guests with warm pungent butter as it did so.

As Ada watched the sauce hit Lucy Borgia, who recoiled in horror.

'No-o-o-o-o!' she screamed as she turned and fled from the room.

For a moment nobody spoke.

MacDuff picked up a napkin and wiped his face.

'As Dr Jensen says, when a man is tired of garlic butter, he is tired of life.'

Chapter Twelve

Nobody noticed Ada leave the dining room. They were too busy throwing food at each other and arguing at the top of their voices.

Ada hurried up the grand staircase, her heels clicketty-clacking on the steps as she did so. When she reached Lucy Borgia's room she found her governess lying motionless on the bed.

She was wearing a black slip, and her black dress lay crumpled in the corner.

'I'm sorry, Ada,' she said weakly, 'I failed you . . . but the garlic . . . it is poison to vampires . . .'

'It was an accident,' said Ada. 'You did your best.'

'Please, take that away from here. The smell . . .' Lucy pointed to her black dress. 'At least the garlic didn't touch my umbrella . . .'

Ada picked up the dress.

'Now I must rest,' said Lucy, closing her eyes,

'to regain my strength. I'm afraid it is up to you now, Ada. You must stop Maltravers and rescue those poor creatures!'

Ada left Lucy's room and slid down the banister. Reaching the first-floor landing, she saw a familiar, flickering glow.

'Ishmael,' she said, noting how extra see-through the ghost of a mouse looked, 'what's wrong?'

'I've just come from the broken wing,' said Ishmael, his whiskers trembling, 'where I overheard Maltravers talking to one of your father's guests.'

'Which one?' asked Ada, getting down from the banister and walking with Ishmael along the corridor to her room.

'Cruel eyes, pointy moustache, big chin . . .' said the mouse. 'I didn't like him.'

'Von Hellsung,' said Ada, entering her enormous bedroom and closing the door behind her.

Ishmael stood on the Anatolian

carpet and looked up at her with wide eyes.

'They've got it all planned out. Tomorrow night, for the indoor hunt, Maltravers has laid out a route through the broken wing that leads up to the rooftops.'

'The rooftops?' said Ada, puzzled. 'But my father wouldn't have agreed to that. He never goes up to the rooftops, not since the night my mother . . .' she paused.

'The man with the cruel eyes laughed and said that that way none of them could escape.' Ishmael shuddered. 'He said that the heads would look splendid on the wall of his hunting lodge in Bavaria*.'

'The heads?' said Ada, sitting down on the edge of her eight-poster bed. 'This is even worse than I had imagined . . .'

'That's what I thought,' said Ishmael. 'What shall we do?'

Ada kicked off the slippers with the

*Rupert von Hellsung's hunting lodge, the Sinister Schloss, is located in the spooky forests of the Bavarian Alps. As well as the heads of stags, boars and bears on the walls, Von Hellsung also keeps a stuffed English hedgehog called Mrs Tiggiewinkle in a glass case by the door.

clicketty-clack heels and slipped on her black pumps.

'There's only one thing we can do . . .' she said thoughtfully.

'And what's that?' asked Ishmael.

Ada's green eyes sparkled. 'Call a meeting of the Attic Club!' she said.

The next morning Ada overslept. It was Saturday, the day of the annual metaphorical bicycle race and indoor hunt. Poor Ada had been up half the night.

She climbed out of bed and went into her dressing room, where she found her Saturday clothes laid out on the Dalmatian divan. She got dressed quickly in the crimson velvet jacket with gold buttons and the white damask dress, together with the dark green cape, and picked up the pearl-handled umbrella next to it.

Ignoring her big clumpy boots, Ada put on her black leather pumps and slipped quietly out of the room as the great-uncle clock on the mantelpiece struck twelve.

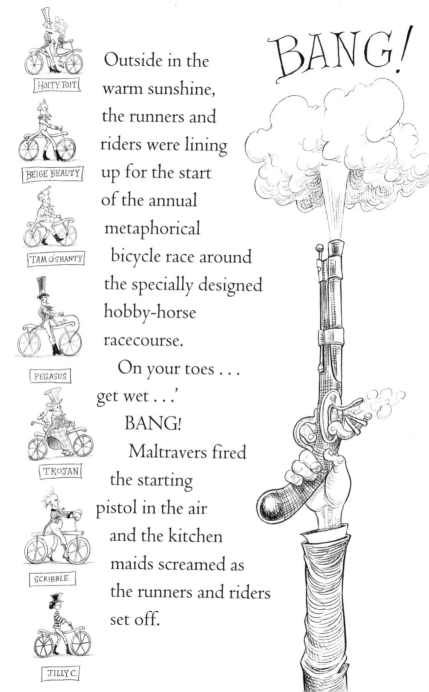

HOITY-TOIT

BEIGE BEAUTY

TAM O'SHANTY

PEGASUS

TROJAN

SCRIBBLE

JILLY C.

Outside in the warm sunshine, the runners and riders were lining up for the start of the annual metaphorical bicycle race around the specially designed hobby-horse racecourse.

On your toes ... get wet ...'

BANG!

Maltravers fired the starting pistol in the air and the kitchen maids screamed as the runners and riders set off.

BANG!

1.

Round the first bend, Lady George and Tristram on Hoity-Toit were in the lead, followed closely by Lord Goth on Pegasus, the poets Molebridge and O'Quincy on Beige Beauty and Tam O'Shanty side by side, then Dr Jensen and MacDuff on Trojan with Mary Shellfish on Jilly C., and Martin Puzzlewit on Scribble bringing up the rear.

2.

Up the Hill of Ambition, Hoity-Toit, Beige Beauty and Tam O'Shanty slipped back on the muddy path, and Lord Goth took the lead.

3.

Down the other side, Dr Jensen rapidly gained speed, Trojan knocking Beige Beauty and Tam O'Shanty out of the way and sending the two poets head first into the Pond of Introspection.

On the Gravel Path of Conceit, Lady George
lost a shoe and Tristram fell off the back of
the tandem and tore his shirt cuff.

Racing towards the Slough of Despond,
the remaining riders rapidly slowed as the
wheels of their hobby horses got clogged
with mud. Dr Jensen scooped up a handful
and hurled it at Martin Puzzlewit behind
him. With a high-pitched scream of outrage,
the radical cartoonist fell off Scribble
and sank up to his middle in a slurry-filled
puddle.

Three riders now remained as the race reached
the Avenue of Outrageous Fortune: Dr Jensen,
shaking the mud from the hems of his huge tartan
trousers; Lord Goth, bespattered but elegantly
determined, and Mary Shellfish, clinging on to
her hobby horse.

As they entered the tunnel of trees, Dr Jensen swerved across Lord Goth's path. MacDuff reached out from the basket sidecar and tried to stick his club into the spokes of Pegasus. Just in time, his legs a blur of movement, Lord Goth zigzagged away.

MacDuff's club clattered along the trunks of the trees, dislodging several squirrels, which fell into his basket. He let out a piercing shriek and leaped into Dr Jensen's lap, causing the doctor to steer into a tree with a resounding crash.

Lord Goth and Mary Shellfish rounded the last bend and galloped towards the finishing post neck and neck. Suddenly, swooping down out of a clear blue sky, a large seabird swooped down and dropped a lump of ice down the neck of Mary Shellfish's Breton smock.

With an indignant yelp the distinguished lady novelist ploughed into the Chicane of Thwarted Hope and fell off her hobby horse.

Raising his top hat in elegant triumph, Lord Goth and Pegasus cantered past the finishing post to be greeted by the cheers of the grooms and housemaids.

Coming from the old icehouse and rounding the corner of the west wing, Ada paused. She held a portfolio in one hand and an umbrella in the other, which she used to wave to Arthur Halford. The hobby-horse groom nodded in reply.

Then Ada turned and hurried across the Venetian terrace before disappearing through the Byzantine windows into Ghastly-Gorm Hall.

Chapter Thirteen

As darkness fell over Ghastly-Gorm Hall a procession of villagers from the nearby hamlet of Gormless made their way in through the gates and down the drive. Flaming torches in hand, they quietly filed around the overly ornamental

fountain and trooped around the side of the
west wing at the back of the house.

There, amidst the weeds and tangled
undergrowth of the Back of Beyond Garden
(unfinished), the crowd of villagers peered
through the dusty windows of the broken wing as
they waited for the indoor hunt to begin.

Meanwhile, in the main hall of Ghastly-Gorm,
Lord Goth and his guests assembled on their
hobby horses.

Molebridge and O'Quincy still weren't speaking to each other. Sitting astride their hobby horses, holding long-handled butterfly nets, the two poets glared at each other.

On their tandem, Hoity-Toit, Lady George and Tristram shared an extra-long-handled butterfly net and were very excited.

'I do so enjoy chasing miniature pheasant,' Lady George was saying to Lord Goth. In the saddle behind her, Tristram nodded enthusiastically.

'Maltravers has just told me he has a surprise in store for us,' said Lord Goth drily.

Although he didn't show it, Lord Goth was delighted with his victory in the metaphorical bicycle race, and had high hopes for the indoor hunt.

'As Dr Jensen says, when a man is tired of surprises, he's tired of life,' said MacDuff from his seat in the basket sidecar attached to the doctor's hobby horse.

Dr Jensen poked Martin Puzzlewit with the end of his long-handled butterfly net. The radical cartoonist gripped the handlebars of his hobby horse with his boxing-gloved fists and tried hard not be provoked.

Next to him, Mary Shellfish patted back her carefully coiffured hair and fluttered her eyelashes at Rupert von Hellsung.

'I hope you're not still cold,' she said with a girlish giggle, as she looked at the ankle-length bearskin cape von Hellsung was wearing, 'After all, this is an indoor hunt, you know.'

'Indeed,' said von Hellsung who, much to Lord Goth's disappointment, had excused himself from the metaphorical bicycle race due to a sudden 'chill'.

'Now I am recovered, I am very much looking forward to a successful hunt,' he said, sitting forward in the saddle of his hobby horse, the Ride of the Valkyrie.

Maltravers stepped out from behind the Bruges

tapestry, a bunch of keys in one hand and a huntsman's horn in the other. He shook the keys theatrically.

'I have released this year's quarry!' he announced. 'Let the indoor hunt begin!'

Maltravers raised the horn to his mouth and blew hard.

Lord Goth and his guests leaped forward on their hobby horses, galloped though the doorway to the broken wing and clattered down the flight of stairs on the other side before charging down the dark cobwebby corridor beyond.

'Tally who?'

'Tally what?'

'Tally where?'

The cries went up as they set about exploring the corridors, hallways and passages.

Maltravers, though, had left nothing to chance.

Daubed on the walls at helpful intervals were messages with arrows that read, 'This way', 'Turn left', 'Turn right' and 'Carry on till the next junction'.

As Lord Goth and his guests clattered along the corridors, they caught glimpses of feathered creatures fluttering ahead and heard the clatter of fleeing hooves and odd wild ape-like grunts echoing through the broken wing.

Floorboards had been pulled up and laid on the stairs to allow the hobby horses to trundle up them in pursuit of the indoor game, which fled upward just ahead of the pursuing guests. Flashes of orange fur and glimpses of bright green feathers and golden claws only served to spur the indoor hunt onward as the riders waved their butterfly nets wildly above their heads. Outside the watching villagers cheered and waved their flaming torches as they strained to see the shadowy shapes through the filthy windows.

Higher and higher the creatures and their pursuers went, up staircases prepared for them by the indoor gamekeeper. As the indoor hunt neared the upper levels of the broken wing, Lord Goth on Pegasus fell back in dismay.

Finally the indoor hunt arrived on a landing with a large sign daubed on the wall that read, 'This way straight ahead'. Von Hellsung galloped forward and burst through the door in front of them. The others followed and found themselves on the rooftops of the broken wing. A forest of chimney stacks stretched out before them and the dome of Ghastly-Gorm Hall rose up behind, dark against the moonlit sky. Below, the torches of the watching villagers twinkled.

Lord Goth galloped through the doorway in last place and fell trembling to his knees. Pegasus clattered down on to the tiles as Lord Goth released his grip on the handlebars. His guests turned and stared at him.

When Lord Goth looked up his handsome face was wet with tears. His magnificent hair fluttered in the breeze and his brooding eyebrows knitted into a sorrowful frown.

'Parthenope,' he breathed, 'So headstrong, so wilful, so wild. That is why I fell in love with you and why I couldn't stop you from coming up here to walk the roof ridges . . . oh, but that night! The thunder! The lightning! . . . The horror, the horror . . .'

'There they are!' shouted Rupert von Hellsung, pointing excitedly.

Sitting on the ornamental chimneys a little way off were eight extraordinary creatures seemingly frozen in terror – a Siren, three harpies, a faun, a centaur and two great apes.

Lady George, Tristram, the poets, Dr Jensen, MacDuff and Mary Shellfish raised their butterfly nets, only for von Hellsung to push them roughly aside.

'They're mine!' he roared, throwing back his bearskin cape to reveal two quadruple-barrelled hunting pistols in calf leather holsters strapped to his belt.

On one holster the word 'Hansel' was stamped in raised letters; on the other, 'Gretel'.

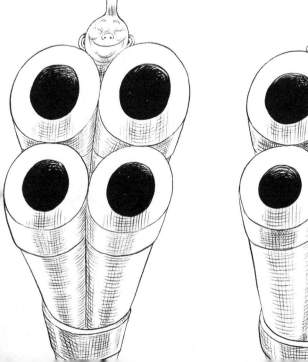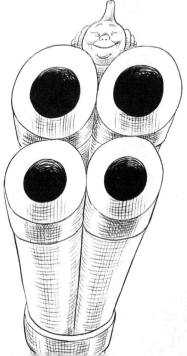

As the others
watched, stunned,
von Hellsung drew
the hunting pistols and
fired –
once,
twice, four
times, eight
times . . . With
each deadly
shot, one of the
creatures shattered
in front of the
onlookers.
Von Hellsung
holstered Hansel and
Gretel with a delighted
grin and drew a long serrated
hunting sword from his belt.
'Now for the heads!'
he said, as he strode across
the rooftop to the row of

chimneys but then he stopped dead in his tracks.

'What's this?' he roared.

At his feet was a pile of broken ice.

At that moment Ada stepped out from behind an ornamental chimney a little way further off. The Siren Sesta was by her side.

From the chimneys around her, the other members of the Attic Club emerged, each with a creature. Ruby the outer-pantry maid stood next to Mr Omalos the faun. Emily Cabbage had a harpy on each arm and one perched on her head. Kingsley the chimney caretaker was arm in arm with the Wife of Barnes, and Arthur Halford was holding hands with the Wildman of Putney while William Cabbage patted Hamish the Shetland centaur on his shaggy head.

'I will have my trophies!' shrieked von Hellsung, leaping up on to a chimney pot and jumping across to another, swinging his hunting sword wildly as he advanced across the rooftop.

'Rupert von Hellsung, we meet at last,' came a soft lilting voice with the hint of an accent. Lucy Borgia stepped out from behind a chimney stack and raised an umbrella. The gold tip glinted in the moonlight.

'How dare you . . . !' von Hellsung began, slashing at the governess with his sword, only for Lucy Borgia to take three steps back, pirouette on top of a chimney pot and lightly but firmly nudge her assailant in the middle of his tummy with the tip of her umbrella.

Losing his balance, von Hellsung teetered for a moment before toppling like a felled fir tree down the chimney on which he'd been standing. A series of bumps and crashes followed, together with shrieks of pain and indignation getting fainter and fainter until a final muffled thump.

'He'll have landed in the Bathroom of Zeus, I reckon,' said Kingsley the chimney caretaker with a knowing glance down the chimney. 'Well played, Ada!'

Ada blushed.

'I couldn't have done it without you,' she said, 'without all of you.'

A huge figure loomed up behind her wearing a sea captain's hat and a sailcloth coat. On his shoulder was perched an albatross. The Polar Explorer opened his wooden trunk and, moving his spare foot* to one side, handed Emily Cabbage the watercolours she'd done of the Siren and the others.

'Thank you,' he said. 'These were a great help.'

'Your ice sculptures were beautiful,' said Emily, taking the paintings. 'I'm so sorry they had to be destroyed.'

'I'll have plenty of time to do more,' said the Polar Explorer, turning towards Mary Shellfish, who'd gone very pale and was trembling uncontrollably. 'After I've had a little chat with Mary about this so-called novel of hers . . .'

Foot Note

*The Polar Explorer's spare foot is kept in his wooden trunk and only used if absolutely necessary. At the present time, the spare foot is using the extensive knowledge of its former owner, a distinguished historian, to write footnotes to a Gothic novel.

He held up a leather-bound volume in a black-fingernailed hand.

'Water, water everywhere, nor any drop to drink!' squawked the albatross.

'I was going to share all the proceeds with you, dear monster,' Mary Shellfish simpered. 'I just wasn't sure where you lived . . .'

Lord Goth got unsteadily to his feet and looked across the rooftops to where Ada and her friends were standing. His eyes met Ada's and this time they didn't fill with sadness, and he didn't look away.

'My dear brave daughter,' he said, holding his arms out wide.

Ada rushed into them and Lord Goth closed his arms around her.

'You really are like your beautiful mother!' he said. 'Brave, intrepid and graceful!'

Lord Goth turned to the creatures. 'There seems to have been an awful misunderstanding,' he said in his quiet yet elegant voice. 'I can only apologize. Please, accept my hospitality and the

hospitality of Ghastly-Gorm Hall.'

'My harpies and I would be honoured,' said Siren Sesta.

'We'd love to, wouldn't we, Hamish?' said Mr Omalos, and the Wildman of Putney and the Wife of Barnes looked at Lord Goth with a sad but grateful expression in their eyes.

Lord Goth picked up his hobby horse and turned to his guests. 'It has been an unusual hunt this year, and I'll be having words with my indoor game-keeper,' he said, then looked at his daughter and smiled. 'But a memorable indoor hunt for all that.'

The guests agreed.

In the distance, a Bavarian coach with a sooty Rupert von Hellsung inside raced through the gates of Ghastly-Gorm Hall and disappeared into the night.

week later, as a bright silver moon rose above the great dome of Ghastly-Gorm Hall, the Attic Club met for a midnight picnic against the ornamental chimney stacks. Ruby the outer-pantry maid had brought cucumber cupcakes and strawberry iced tea, while Arthur Halford demonstrated his harness for safely climbing up chimney pots. Kingsley the chimney caretaker did a tap dance at the top of the tallest chimney and everyone clapped. William blended in with the brickwork while Emily painted a watercolour of the moon over the dome.

'Now it is my turn,' said Ada. 'I've been practising, with Arthur and Kingsley's help . . .' She blushed. Strung between two ornamental chimneys was a rope, which Arthur had safely secured, together with a safety net. Kingsley handed Ada a pole with a chimney brush on each end and helped her on to the tightrope. Ada was

wearing her mother's tightrope-walking slippers.
Slowly and carefully she walked the tightrope,
balancing with the pole as she did so.

Halfway between the two chimneys she
paused, silhouetted against the bright moon.

Below, on the rooftop, the Attic Club cheered.
Ada took a bow.

Epilogue

It was Mary Shellfish who had given Ada the idea. Her bestselling novel *The Monster, or Prometheus Misbehaves* had been published by a Mr Macmillan in London, allowing the Polar Explorer's life and adventures to reach a wide and appreciative audience. Despite their slight misunderstanding, the lady novelist and the monster had parted on good terms and the Polar Explorer had promised to tell Mary Shellfish all about his ex-girlfriend for her next novel.

Ada said goodbye to the Siren Sesta, the harpies, Mr Omalos and Hamish the Shetland centaur, who'd all returned safely to their homes without any ill feeling once Lord Goth had explained that he'd known nothing of the invitations that Maltravers had sent. They had enjoyed the hospitality of Ghastly-Gorm Hall, staying in the west wing and having the run of the grounds for the rest of their visit.

As for Maltravers, he'd apologized for the invitations and told Lord Goth that he had only wanted the indoor hunt to be unusual this year and had had no idea of von Hellsung's actual intentions. He claimed that he hadn't meant the creatures any harm and that he'd been as much misled as everyone else. Ada didn't believe him, but Lord Goth was so honourable and fair that he'd given the indoor gamekeeper the benefit of the doubt.

Ada didn't trust Maltravers one little bit and, from the

look the indoor gamekeeper gave her as he sloped out of Lord Goth's study after a severe telling off, she could tell the feeling was mutual.

Life had returned to normal, only better than before. Ada didn't have to wear the big, clumpy boots any more and she could see her father whenever she wanted to. Lord Goth had finally come to terms with the terrible tragedy of her mother's accident, it seemed, and was trying to make it up to Ada. And Maltravers kept himself to himself, at least for the time being.

But there was still the ghost of a mouse who appeared on the Anatolian carpet each night, and who was happy for Ada but still sad about being a ghost.

And then Ada had an idea.

She went to her father's study and went inside. Lord Goth was in the grounds on Pegasus, but Ada knew he wouldn't mind. She crossed to the wall behind her father's desk and knelt down at the skirting board. There, nibbled through the wood, was Ishmael's mousehole.

Ada reached inside and felt around. Sure enough her fingers closed round a tiny bundle of papers. Taking them out, she carefully folded them into a letter and took it to Arthur Halford to send to London on the Gormless mail coach. The letter was addressed to Mr Macmillan the publisher.

That night, as the sun was setting, Ada heard a little sigh. Turning round from the window she saw Ishmael twinkling palely on the Anatolian carpet.

'Thank you, Ada,' he said, when she told him what she had done, 'Now there's nothing keeping me here any more.' He floated up and out of the window. 'I think I can go now.'

He looked back at Ada and smiled. 'Remember me . . .' he said.

Ada watched as Ishmael walked into the beautiful sunset and went towards the light.

'I will,' she said.